LIFE IS FINE

ALSO BY ALLISON WHITTENBERG

SWEET THANG

LIFE IS FINE

allison whittenberg

delacorte press

Published by Delacorte Press
an imprint of Random House Children's Books
a division of Random House, Inc.
New York

Delacorte Press and colophon are registered trademarks of
Random House, Inc.

Visit us on the Web! www.randomhouse.com/teens

Educators and librarians, for a variety of teaching tools,
visit us at www.randomhouse.com/teachers

Library of Congress Cataloging-in-Publication Data
Whittenberg, Allison.
Life is fine / by Allison Whittenberg.—1st ed.
p. cm.
Summary: With a neglectful mother who has an abusive, live-in
boyfriend, life for fifteen-year-old Samara is not fine, but when a
substitute teacher walks into class one day and introduces her to poetry,
she starts to view life from a different perspective.
ISBN 978-0-385-73480-6 (trade)—ISBN 978-0-385-90478-0 (lib. ed.)
[1. Child abuse—Fiction. 2. Mothers and daughters—Fiction.
3. Interpersonal relations—Fiction. 4. African Americans—Fiction.
5. Philadelphia (Pa.)—Fiction.] I. Title.
PZ7.W6179Li2008
[fic]—dc22
2007027604

The text of this book is set in 12-point Goudy.

Printed in the United States of America

10 9 8 7 6 5 4 3 2 1

First Edition

LIFE IS FINE

one

There comes a point in every relationship when verbal communication becomes unnecessary. For us, the connection was something that grew over time, but looking back, there were early clues. The first time I saw him, our eyes met and locked, and the air was charged with electricity. I didn't even notice the glass between us.

I had been seeing him for about a year now, often skipping school to get to him before visiting hours were up. His name was Dru. He was short (only five feet), but he had long, thin arms and large, powerful hands. But his eyes were what hooked me. They were hooded and on the small side, but dreamily deep-set. I knew he'd be happier out of captivity. He'd be pleased living up in a tree, hoot-barking in his natural element in Indonesia. Instead, like me, he'd been born in Philadelphia.

Dru still lived with his mom. On this particular day, she was farther back in the cell and, as usual, left us alone.

He talked to me with those eyes, those hooded eyes.

"What's up?" he asked.

"Not much," I answered.

Dru was an ape. I'm not speaking metaphorically. I'm referring to his burnt-orange hair and his simian heritage.

But I'm kind of an animal, too. A chameleon. I blend into the scenery. I have to. I hate attention. At school, the popular girls wear barn red lipstick and low-slung jeans. I'm always more bundled and layered than the weather dictates. I think of it as protection. My black hair hangs straight, parted down the middle and curled in just a little at the bone of my chin. I wear black or brown pants with black or brown shirts.

The announcement came on saying that time was up.

Dru and I bade our visual farewells.

The gold October sun was high as I ducked out of the primate center. I bypassed the fruit bat and the flamingo. I overlooked the Komodo dragon and the kookaburra.

Outside the zoo, the world churned and bubbled with agitation. It was rush hour. The bus stop was crowded with people. A group of girls swayed to the beat coming from a boom box. An older woman read a dog-eared Bible.

"Damn, why you looking so evil?" A nearby toothless man tried to make me smile.

But he only made me frown more. I hate to act on demand.

I had a window seat. Around Girard Avenue, I looked out and saw a man peeing on a tree. He was ordinary otherwise, a young man in a sweatshirt and blue jeans. The city has a way of being so public it's private. Maybe he thought he was in the seclusion of his bathroom. Or maybe he just couldn't hold it and didn't want to have to pay. A lot of stores won't let you use their facilities if you don't buy something first.

The bus let me off four blocks from my house. There were For Sale signs all over my neighborhood. None of the houses were particularly big, so they weren't much to take care of. Yet they had gotten shabbier and shabbier as the years melted on. Grids of black metal bars over the windows and doors were their only home improvements.

Paint peeled and no one repainted. Shutters and shingles fell and no one replaced them. Then in came these outsiders, and they bought the houses for a song.

Drug dealers cooperated with this buyout and kindly moved their business elsewhere.

When I got to my house, I lit a cigarette and inhaled deeply. I hunched in the doorway before entering. I had to mentally prepare myself to go inside. When I did, CD cases snapped under my feet. Magazines, junk mail, various sections of the newspaper, and stacks of catalogs were all over the floor of the living room. There were crumbs on the end tables and scuffs on the wall. The banister needed painting.

I would go days without seeing or hearing from my mom. On average, she worked sixty hours a week. As a consolation prize, I got Q.

A grown man named after a letter.

He was eight years younger than my mom and eight years older than me. He was how Mom got her groove back.

But I'd been po'd at Q for the past two years. Mom had known him for only seven weeks before he came moving on in. (Great example, Mom.)

Now he rested on the couch with his cotton-socked feet on the coffee table. Why wear shoes? Where did he have to go?

As far as I could tell, he was not trained in anything. My mom was his only means of support.

He would lie on the couch, snacking on pork rinds and Mountain Dew. The way Q snacked, he should have weighed three thousand pounds. Instead, he was wiry like a worm.

He had a daughter somewhere I had heard him mention once or twice. I think she was five or six. Anyway, he never visited her.

They say it's nice to have a man around the house. Yet the last time there was a power outage, I was the one standing on a stepladder fiddling with the circuit breaker.

The TV blared *Judge Mathis*. Q looked up at me icily. I glared back at him. We'd gotten out of the habit of speaking to each other a long time ago.

I hated him.

He didn't contribute to the household but easily got more use out of the place than either Mom or I. He was always watching cable TV or opening the refrigerator door. He was really icky to look at. He had large pores and more acne than most people my age. But it wasn't his downright homeliness I resented. I hated his *thereness*.

Mom didn't care how much I disliked Q. She had her own life to lead, as she told me on the occasions when I spoke with her.

I didn't know my father. I believed I should, for

6

medical history if nothing else. The old saying wasn't true. Ignorance wasn't bliss.

Maybe my somewhere father didn't know I existed. Maybe that was why he never contacted me with a phone call or a postcard or an e-mail. By land, air, or sea.

I'd been up against Q for the past two years. And before Q, there was someone worse.

Sometimes I imagined I came from a loving family. A biscuit-baking mom, a nine-to-five wage-slave father, and two sisters, one younger and one older. Or maybe they could both be younger, but not by too much of a gap. This imaginary family included a dog, a collie named Schulley. Each afternoon, my mom and dad would ask me about my day. I'd blow them off because I needed my space.

"Honey, are you upset about something? Do you want to talk about it?" my pretend mom would say.

"I'm busy," I'd call over my shoulder, closing the bedroom door behind me. As for my two

sisters (let's call them Claudia and Denise), they loved me so much they were always hanging out in my room, but who had time for them? I'd be dating a cool-as-hell dropout. I'd ride on the back of his motorcycle and clutch him like a caterpillar.

Instead of being met by my ideal family, that evening, like so many others, I was stuck heating a frozen burrito at dinnertime for my one-thousandth meal alone.

Life was really something. I often thought maybe I should read one of those self-help books. With assisted knowledge, I might easily conclude that the first fifteen years of my life were crap, but maybe, just maybe, the next fifteen years would be better.

I needed a thing, something to lean on. I felt like abusing a drug, but I didn't know which. Or developing an eating disorder, but I didn't know how. Being in love with an orangutan was the only monkey on my back.

I figured I could up my smoking habit. I pinched

cigarettes from my mom. If she noticed, she never said.

Another year down the toilet.

I hated my life in this cluttered, hollow house. I should have had my own life, but I didn't. All I had was Dru, an orangutan. That was it.

two

The next morning, I hit the snooze button seven times. The day was beginning without me, but I really didn't care.

I was late for school, and I was sent directly to the guidance counselor, Bowman. He was a short man, starting to go a little around the waist, but otherwise lanky, even stern looking. He sat in a green imitation-leather armchair.

When he asked me about my poor attendance, I said nothing.

He shuffled through my file and told me to speak up for myself.

"I don't have anything to say," I said.

"That's counterproductive," he said. "Just sitting there with no explanation. You've crossed the threshold. You've been absent fourteen times so far."

I dug in my knapsack and pulled out a cigarette.

"Put that away," he told me.

I flicked my lighter till it produced a flame.

"Put it away," he repeated.

"Can I ask you a question first?" I inquired, holding the fire to the cigarette's end.

"What's your question?" He frowned.

I took a draw. "Mind if I smoke?"

He took the cigarette from my lips. He held it like it was poisonous before depositing it in the trash.

"It's just a question."

"Do you want to pass? Do you want to get through this?" He wagged his finger at me. "You keep treating this lightly and you'll find the joke is on you. You'll find your whole life has passed you by."

He sounded pissed. Like I had hurt him personally. I rolled my eyes. The last thing I needed was a five-minute father.

"You're right," I said, rising as if inspired. "I've seen the light. I'm going to try out for the glee club, the cheerleading squad, and maybe even the football team!"

Back in the halls, things were noisy with all the roars and rumbles and calls and cries. Kids ran around. It was all so surreal, a mosaic of faces that meant nothing to me. All my life I'd been lonely. It's like I was genetically predisposed. I don't remember playing jacks or marbles with anyone, even. There are some people who are popular, who everyone else gloms on to. Then there are those who are jeered at. Then there are the anonymous ones like me, who attract only sporadic concern from the guidance counselor.

My first period was English, the easiest class in the history of high school. Krista Flanders never worked us to the bell or even near it. She always gave us class time to do homework. She was so lax, she once came to class in flip-flops, like she'd just arrived from some beach in Wildwood.

Just as I sat down the weird girl who didn't wear a bra walked in. She took a seat by the wall. I never knew what her outfits were trying to say. I think it's called punk when you wear safety pins, leather jackets, tight black pants, and T-shirts with British bands on them. Blue was the color of choice for her lipstick and hair, which cut quite a contrast with her medium brown complexion.

My eyes moved to the brainiac in the class, who sat up front and volunteered for things, letting everyone know he was in the room.

It was three minutes past the start of class. Where the hell was Flanders?

I kept my eyes on the door. A man strolled in. He introduced himself as Jerome Halbrook. He placed a "Mr." in front of it. He might as well have put a "sir" before it. At least he didn't say "I'm your substitute today." I rolled my eyes anyway. Though elderly, he didn't seem fragile. You know how some old people walk with a shuffle, slow-moving and sullen? Mr. Jerome Halbrook was energetic. Maybe he was prematurely gray. He was striking and of sharp construction. He had a dark oblong face, and his cheekbones elegantly jutted out.

A few students snickered when they saw him. Dignity intact, he stood proudly at the board.

He wore schoolteacher regalia—a suit and a tie. It occurred to me that he was the only one in the building with a tie on. The principal, Lauter, went only as far as a blazer and jeans. And with those, Lauter left his shirt collar open so his bull neck could breathe.

This Mr. Jerome Halbrook passed out a sheet of paper with a poem on it. We neeeeeever did poetry with Flanders. I didn't think we were missing anything. Poetry was pointless. At least fiction could be turned into a movie. I looked at the clock—only nine minutes down.

Did he really think he was going to occupy us for the whole period with this drek? He asked us to read the poem to ourselves. After we read the poem silently, the sub closed his eyes as if he were about to pray. Then he opened them and began reading aloud. He was a great reader. There was a deep, silken quality to his voice, crawling inside each word, each syllable.

The title of the poem was "To His Coy Mistress," written by someone named Andrew Marvell. It was written as a conversation, though only one person was talking. The main character in the poem, a man, was trying to get a woman to have relations with him. She was shy, and the poem insinuated that she'd never had sex before. She was called "coy" because she was scared. She was also young, I guessed about my age. She was told by her pursuer that life was short, and that if she did not give in right now, she might not have the chance again.

"Carpe diem. Seize the day!" the sub gushed, and he repeated the last line of the poem. " 'Thus, though we cannot make our sun / Stand still, yet we will make him run.' "

I really didn't know high art, but I hardly found this profound. Beauty crumbles into death, and that's what all the makeup ads in those shiny women's magazines never tell you. . . . They try to make you think face cream will stave off the inevitable. A woman is like a flower. Everyone's interested in her when she's young and perky, but when she's old and brittle, one touch and the petals fall, and no one sends her instant messages anymore. Blah, blah, blah.

The substitute kept lauding the classic construction of the poem. Its ingenuity.

Then he went on and on and on and on and on about this being not only one of the best poems ever written, but also his personal favorite.

I couldn't hold it in any longer. "He's just trying to get into her pants," I blurted out.

Every head turned in my direction. There was a splash of laughter.

"What is your name, young lady?" the sub asked.

"Samara," I answered.

"Well, Samara, can you go further with your thought?"

The class was still looking at me hard. I didn't care. It wasn't like I had any friends to lose. "It's obvious that the girl is underage and this old dude is just trying to jump her bones."

"Are you quite certain, Samara, that that is all this poem is about?" he asked me.

"I'm certain that old men want to sleep with young girls," I answered.

With that, the class was really going, and I figured why close the barn door now, the horse is gone. "Why is the girl 'coy' in the first place?" I asked as I pointed to the word on the page. "Maybe she's just not that into him. She has every right to keep her 'quaint honor' and he has no right to suggest that 'worms' will 'try' her 'virginity.' "

"Don't you recognize symbolism?" the brainiac in the front row said to me.

"Virgins are people, not symbols," that weird girl by the wall said.

"You're both taking it too literally," the same boy said.

"The poem says 'let us sport us while we may,' " I argued.

"Yeah, marry the first bum that comes along and live in a trailer park," the weird girl said.

"It's a carpe diem poem, what else is it supposed to say?" asked the brainiac. "It's just like that other one. You know what I'm talking about—" He gestured to the sub. "It starts, 'Gather ye rosebuds.' "

" 'To the Virgins, to Make Much of Time.' 'For

having lost but once your prime / You may for-ever tarry.' "

"What's 'tarry'?" a girl in row three with her hair in a loose knot asked.

"Wait," the smart guy answered. "The poet warns the girl that she may be waiting forever."

"Talk about a full-court press," the weird girl said. "These horny guys will have you believing they are the last men on earth."

The class really laughed at that. Laughter hung in the air like smoke. Some people clapped. We never had a discussion like this with Flanders.

"Back to the poem, what if I were to tell you that this poem alludes to the great era of exploration in England and the popular fascination with the East?" the sub asked.

For the next several minutes, our words chased down that alley. We spoke of how at the time of Marvell's poem, which was published in 1681, the sun never set on the British Isles. That tiny country was able to stretch its tentacles of influence to affect the entire world.

But it wasn't long before our textual analysis swerved back to the idea that the poem is really about sex.

"The feeling of bliss can disappear, and what is left is your heart, which contains your true feelings," the AP wannabe said.

"All the poem talks about is the beauty of her skin and her body," the weird girl said.

"Exactly," I said.

"It's just a game he's talking. This man desires something, and he will do anything to get it."

"That's right," I agreed.

"Like an animal hunts its prey," the weird girl insisted.

The substitute's eyes glinted with satisfaction at all the discussion he had inspired.

"Just like an animal will do when it needs to eat and get its prey to satisfy its hunger. This man wants the mistress to satisfy his desires," I said.

The bell rang. Time was up already.

The rest of my class periods sucked.
I hated Algebra II.

I hated psychology.

I hated history.

Study hall was okay.

Freedom came at 2:24. I rushed to my locker to deposit my books. Someone tapped my shoulder.

"You were great."

I spun around. "What?"

It was that weird girl. She looked weird even up close. She had dimples. They asserted themselves as she smiled. "You exposed Andrew Marvell, that sexist-pig poet—"

"Who?" I asked.

"The writer of the poem this morning."

"Oh, right."

"Are you a feminist?" she asked me.

"No," I answered dully. "Baptist."

three

There are some people who are like paddles upon water. Their impression vanishes in moments. Then there are those who linger. I thought of that sub as I made my decision not to go to school the next day. I weighed the pros and cons and decided that since that was just one class and there were five others I'd have to put up with, it wasn't worth it.

Whatever pangs of regret I might have had were staved off because I wasn't even sure he was going to be there. He was a substitute, after all. Once at the zoo, I was confident that I had made the right choice. I really didn't want to see anyone else at school, and I was quite certain nobody really wanted to see me.

The zoo had been thick with people during the summer months, but now, during fall, the crowd was thin. I was faithful to this nearly deserted place, which was still colorful and loud, with the geese honking. I wasn't interested in the reptile house with its boa constrictors or the big cat exhibit with its lions and snow leopards. I breezed past the yawning hippopotamuses. My thoughts were only of Dru.

But when I got to his cage, I was disappointed to see that there was another person there.

Dru's lanky arms scratched his crown with his long fingers, and the visitor scratched his head.

The visitor was right up on the glass, with large forward-facing eyes. He was skinny. He seemed to rattle in his jacket.

When Dru hunched his shoulders, so did the visitor. Then the visitor dictated the action. He swished his dreadlocks and Dru shook his fur.

The visitor pounded his feet on the ground and so did Dru. Then the man started flailing like he was being electrocuted. He was stricken with madness, making animal screams. Dru started freaking out like he was having a seizure.

This man was going ape. And he was making my orangutan go ape as well.

Maybe this visitor could feel my stare, my horror.

Our eyes met for a prolonged moment. He stepped toward me and opened his mouth to speak. But I panicked and quickly exited.

I took the number 7 back to my house, not daring to look back until I was safely on the road.

During the ride home, I saw a man peeing. A different man from the last time. He was whizzing in plain view as he walked an incline on the side of the Family Court building. This guy was different, older, old enough to know better. A security guard followed him.

The wrong animals were behind bars.

I leaned back in my seat. Instead of getting scared out of the zoo by some stranger, I could have been hearing sexist poetry with that old sub. I sighed—another missed opportunity.

four

That next day, I found myself at a bookstore. Bookstores have become the new libraries. People sat on the chairs, couches, even footstools flipping pages, wetting their thumbs, their eyes moving along the lines of print. One guy had a stack of a dozen or so books at a center table in the store's café. No coffee. No muffin. He was just reading away like he was in his living room.

Coffeehouses tell loiterers to roll if they try that.

But it's not like I was any better. I was just there to mooch a look at Andrew Marvell and some self-help books.

In the poetry section, the "M"s were on the tippy-top. You'd have to be a monkey to reach that far up. I wondered what Dru was up to as I balanced on a footstool. When I found a collection of Marvell's work, I noticed that it was thicker than a Bible. I just wanted to see what Marvell's other poems were like, not change my religion.

Out of the corner of my eye, I caught sight of a man with a trim mustache and neat clothes, a crease in his trousers and everything. It was him, the substitute.

I decided to scrap my book hunt. I tried for a smooth retreat. I wished I had dark glasses or a hat—a big one with a wide brim that I could pull down—or a paper bag.

Quickly and quietly, I put Marvell back on the shelf.

I glanced back at the sub, wondering if he was still there, before turning to leave.

"Samara?" he asked.

Crap, I thought. "Hello."

He smiled at me with his blue eyes.

"I see I piqued your interest." He gestured to the poetry shelves.

"I was just browsing."

"You missed class."

"I can't go out when it's below forty-five degrees," I lied in a rush. "I have a condition."

"It wasn't particularly cold yesterday."

"I must have gotten a bad weather report. . . . What are you doing here? It seems like you would have read everything already."

"I like to see what's new."

He held up his copy of *The Sonnets of Shakespeare*. I didn't know literature, but even I knew that William Shakespeare had been dead for the last billion years. The sub put it back into the bag. "And sometimes my copies wear out. Did you want to purchase anything?" he asked.

"No, really, I was just looking."

"Are you sure?" he asked, pulling out his wallet. "I have a few extra dollars. I feel a little obliged since I contributed to your addiction."

"Addiction?"

"I know an avid reader when I'm in the presence of one."

"Me?" I was nearly floored by the accusation. He further discombobulated me by suggesting we grab lunch.

We walked past the pizza parlor, the General Nutrition Center, and the lingerie boutique to a diner on the corner called Ahab's. Along the way, I asked him where he lived.

"Not too far from here. Rittenhouse Square," he told me as we walked to the next block.

"You must be rich, then," I said, and immediately imagined that he dwelled in the Dorchester, that fancy condo building where you can't own a closet without putting down a half a million. It was so lush there with the doormen dressed like royal guards, with their uniforms.

"It's pricey there, but I think Society Hill's even worse. The rent there gets as high as a kite. Where is it that you live?"

"Bainbridge Street."

"That's over by what used to be Graduate Hospital."

I shook my head. "After. It's south of South Street. New York has SoHo. We have SoSo."

"That's cute."

The hubbub. The diner was full of people: youngish, oldish, well-to-do, middle-of-the-road. Men and women together. Men together. Women together. Me and the sub. All about us the waitresses were hurrying, hurrying, placing fresh settings before us.

"I plan to order a turkey club," he told me.

"What's that?" I asked.

"Don't you young people eat sandwiches?"

"Sure, just the other day I had some peanut butter and jelly."

He shook his head. "That's not a sandwich. There's no art to that. Picture this: one slice of bread toasted, followed by turkey slices and bacon and by another piece of toast and more turkey and bacon and lettuce and tomato and more bread."

"Three slices of bread?" I asked.

"One goes in the middle," he explained.

"That's a lot of bread."

The waitress was at my elbow.

"We'll have two turkey clubs," I told her.

"What kind of bread?" she asked.

"Gee. I don't know. Rye?" I asked.

"Coming right up," the waitress said, taking my guess as a commitment.

The sub looked at me keenly. "Life offers few opportunities to choose exactly what you want. You might as well take advantage of the chance when it presents itself."

I nodded, though I didn't get what he meant. This impromptu lunch rattled me.

When our sandwiches came, I finally understood. They did look regal, almost gaudy, with green and red toothpicks sticking out of each triangle.

He ate precisely. There was something very pure and decent about him, almost naïve. But then again, you have to be naïve to be a substitute teacher.

"I know you're into all those grab-the-day poems, but what's your favorite story?"

"Easy." He finished his bite. " 'The Lady or the Tiger.' "

"Who wrote it?"

"Frank Stockton."

"Should I know that name?"

"He's not Steinbeck." He took the toothpick out of another square.

"Who?"

The Grapes of Wrath."

I frowned. "Now you're just making up stuff."

"And you wonder why I came out of retirement?" He spread his arms wide as he spoke. "This story has everything. A beautiful woman. Justice. Danger."

"Justice?"

" 'The Lady or the Tiger.' It was written a little after the Civil War."

"Oh, circa when you were born." I couldn't resist. He rolled on without acknowledgment.

"The king is despotic. He judges guilt and innocence by placing the accused in a chamber with two doors. Behind one door there is a tiger, and behind the other is a beautiful woman," he continued.

"That king sounds nuts. So what's the plot?"

"This tyrant king finds out that his beloved daughter is seeing a man he considers unworthy of

33

her, so the suitor is placed in the chamber with the two doors. The twist is that the princess knows which door is which."

"So she tells him." I took a bite of my sandwich. The bacon was good and salty and the turkey was thick.

"Maybe," he said, hedging. "The story never says."

"Isn't it obvious? If she loved him, she wouldn't let him get eaten by a lion."

"Tiger," he corrected me, and added, "Because she loves him, she can't let him marry another."

"So he gets eaten," I guessed.

"No."

"So he gets married," I guessed again.

"No."

Abandoning my curiosity, I threw up my hands.

"So he stands there looking at the two doors for the next fifty years and dies of old age."

The sub wore a purely devilish grin. "It's open-ended."

"Open-ended? Your favorite story has an open ending?" I asked incredulously. That story was only for people who enjoyed thinking, I figured. It was like philosophy.

*　*　*

After we left the restaurant, I lit a cigarette by reflex.

"Don't do that," he warned. "It stunts your growth."

"I'm five four," I told him. "That's good enough for me."

"I'm sure you have things planned for the afternoon," he said.

I grinned sarcastically. "I'm sure I have things planned for the afternoon."

"It was nice seeing you." He tipped his hat. "See you Monday."

"See you Monday," I said, and I let the smoke curl out of my nostrils. I watched this ninety-percent-gray-haired man walk away with his jaunty, purposeful swing to his arms.

My eyes followed him till he was at the end of the block. Then I saw him turn the corner on Eighteenth.

Oh, I have a lot to do. So much.

five

I had nothing to do. I was so bored the rest of the weekend that I couldn't wait till Monday. And school. And Mr. Brook. That was the pet name I had thought up. I couldn't wait to use it on him.

In homeroom, I received a note that said the guidance counselor wanted to see me.

I burst into Bowman's office like a hurricane, surprising him during his morning cup of joe. He made a half circle in his swivel chair to face me.

"Don't worry, Bowman, I won't miss any more days." I put both thumbs up. "I'm on the right track."

Bowman's mouth formed a perfect "O."

I ducked out before he could answer.

When I reached the room, my hopes took a dive. The teacher wasn't Mr. Jerome Halbrook in his suit and tie. It was Ms. Krista Flanders in her low-rise jeans and flip-flops. She was diagramming sentences on the board. Boring ones like: "The writer uses a comma to set off a definition, a restatement, or extra information."

With great lament, I sank into my seat. I folded my arms across my chest.

He promised he'd be here.

The AP-wannabe guy was furiously biting the skin around his fingernails.

I felt like constructing a sign: BRING BACK THE SUB.

That weird girl with the blue lipstick sat down next to me. She punched my arm. "Hey, missed you the other day."

I offered a mechanical smile.

She punched my arm again.

I looked over at her and caught sight of her

notebook. The word "Steph'Annie" was etched on the cover.

"Is that how you spell your name?" I asked.

She nodded enthusiastically.

"You must be the only one in the world," I told her.

"Trying to be."

Class had started, but I could barely hear Flanders. She didn't throw her voice like Mr. Brook.

"I'm Steph'Annie Perdomo," the weird girl said brightly.

"I'm Samara Tuttle," I replied, mimicking her enthusiasm.

Steph'Annie confused my mockery with sincerity. She held out her hand for me to shake it.

I did.

My next class sucked. So did the one after that, but around ten-thirty, I passed room 245. I saw him as if he were an apparition. A mirage.

I squinted just to make sure.

He was erasing the blackboard behind the desk.

My hands were trembling as I knocked on the door and said, "Can't get enough of the place?"

"Samara," he said happily as he turned to me.

I stepped in. "It's my open period, too," I lied. I was supposed to be in phys ed. "Do you know that you are the oldest teacher in America?"

"Oh, I'm a youngster. In Maryland, there is a gentleman who is ninety-three years old. He teaches a full load."

"A ninety-three-year-old teacher?" I asked, laughing a bit. He had to be putting me on.

"I saw his story on the nightly news. He started teaching in the 1930s. He did forty-six straight years. He heard about the lack of black teachers in his district and pulled himself out of retirement in the late 1990s."

"At least he was well rested. . . . You know, his age could really come in handy, like for history. He could give a firsthand account of Washington crossing the Delaware."

"He's a chemistry teacher."

"Even better. He was there when Pythagoras thought up his theorem."

He gave me a smile. "That's geometry."

"All right, so he was present when Oppenheimer split the atom in Manhattan."

"The Manhattan Project didn't take place in New York. It was in a New Mexico desert."

"Then why did they call it the Manhattan Project?" I asked.

"You know, I don't know. That might be worth looking up."

"Is that why you came to us? You think we need role models?"

"I always wanted to be a teacher."

I snorted. "So why aren't you a regular one?"

"I went the business route, the so-called practical one. I was a vice president before I retired."

"This must be the mother of all pay cuts."

"I'm doing this to occupy my time."

"Teaching is a time-consuming hobby."

"I've got time. You would make a good teacher, Samara."

My skin prickled. "A teacher?" I asked incredulously. "I'm trying to get out of this place, not stay here for the rest of my life."

He persisted. "It's different when you have a big desk."

I held my ground. "They'd have to give me more than a big desk."

"What do you want to be, Samara?"

"I don't know. . . . Whatever."

"Whatever? What do you think is going to happen in three more years?" he asked.

"I'll graduate."

"Then what?" he asked.

"Then I move."

"Where?"

I shrugged.

"What do your parents have to say?"

"Not much." By reflex, I reached for a cigarette, then waved my hand away from it. "She's busy."

"Your mother's raising you alone?"

That question made me smirk. "You could say that."

He nodded. "Well, it's very hard being a parent."

"Are you one?"

"No."

"By now, you're probably a grandparent."

"I've never had children."

"Oh," I said. "That's interesting. . . . You were married, right?"

"Twice."

I cocked my head. "Maybe the third time will be the charm."

"Anything is possible." He reached into his satchel and took out a book. "Before I forget. Here." He handed me the book *Immortal Poetry*. "I would like you to read this."

I heard the bonging of the church bells as I got off the bus at my stop. I was dreaming of Mr. Brook, and it felt odd-good. Not odd-bad. Though intraspecies relationships are frowned upon (just ask King Kong), intergenerational liaisons are not. They say men mature more slowly than women— maybe not sixty years more slowly, but more slowly nonetheless—and just thinking of Mr. Brook lifted my spirits. But when I opened the door to my house, all the life was sucked out of me.

The whole place smelled like fried burgers. Q was in the kitchen. I could hear the pan hissing with grease.

The living room was a sty, as usual. I quickly collected the stray papers into a little pile and plugged in a vacuum cleaner.

I heard something clang in the next room. It was like waking a lion. Q came running out, roaring at me.

"I'll be done in a second," I told him.

"Get out of here," he told me.

"I can't straighten out my own house?" I asked in a level voice.

"It's not your house," he told me, yanking the cord out of the socket. The spark made him jump back.

"Serves you right," I said.

"What did you say?"

I wanted to say that again, and more, but I kept silent.

"What did you say?" he asked more loudly.

I finally mumbled, "I'm just straightening things up."

"Who asked you to?"

I steeled myself. "No one has to."

He had the cord in his hand like a whip. "Say it again."

I felt a shiver of fear. "I'll vacuum some other time."

"Don't go changing things around here," he told me.

I moved to leave but bent to pick up what littered my path.

"Leave it!" he screamed at me. His eyes narrowed. They went vacant and wild at the same time.

Determined not to show fear, I squared off to him.

"It's an empty wrapper," I said.

He pushed past the vac. His eyes were blazing with anger. He grabbed me in his greasy hands and shoved me against the wall.

I felt a sharp pain in my spine and my head spun, but I was able to make it out of his way before a swing made contact with me.

He came after me but slid on the slick surface of this month's *HM* magazine. All this jostling had caused the periodical pile to fall on the floor. This made him madder. The room twirled as he snatched me again.

He was close to me now, breathing in little gasps, like he'd been running. He told me, "Girl, I could really hurt you."

Then he let me go.

From my bedroom window, I could see the alleyway behind our house. It was littered with broken bottles and bricks. The bottles were mostly from malt liquor. The bricks were from the condemned house that faced our back door.

I had closed my bedroom door, not with a slam, but regular. I lit a cigarette and sat on my bed and smoked it, trying not to think. Of course, before the first exhale, large tears formed in my eyes.

All the alleyway's crap turned to a blur.

A while later, I heard the raspy sound of stockings shuffling outside my door. My mother was a medical assistant. Every now and then, she wore a dress.

She knocked.

I ignored it.

I heard her try the door and command me to open it.

My mother didn't have a particularly loud voice. It was actually rather soft, and I guess in some other circumstance it could be thought of as soothing.

"Samara," she repeated.

I got up and opened the door.

She looked beat. There were bags under her naturally sleepy brown eyes. Her brown skin looked spent. A few gray root strands peeked though her dyed auburn hair.

She let out an exhausted sigh before saying, "Q told me—"

That was where I lost it. " 'Q said.' 'Q said.' Who is he, God?"

"Keep your voice down, Samara."

"All he does is watch talk shows and make a mess in the living room."

She said, "Keep your snide comments to your-self." Her tone now sounded more aggravated than tired.

"Mom, he attacked me. He threw me against the wall—"

"Samara, I've been working all day; I don't want to come home to this."

"All I was trying to do was clean up the room!"

She always said she was going to be a nurse. She took classes at the community college but kept quitting. I didn't really think she would ever get her license.

"There's not a scratch on you." She stepped forward and checked me for injury, quickly once-overing the back of my head. "You're fine."

"You don't know."

"Samara, shut up."

My mom's words were always bitter, like the skin of walnuts.

I went to the far end of the bed and turned my back to her. Her examination was too curt to be thorough. I pulled up my right sleeve and examined the welts on my arm. His handprint had turned polychromatic.

I spun around just as the door was closing. I put

my sleeve back down. I hated her. More than I hated Q. What if one day he broke my arm? What would she do about that? Further lecture me about how I caused trouble, take Q out for all-you-can-eat shrimp at Red Lobster while I set my own bone in a cast?

I'd been sort of abused by Q for a while. But it wasn't the kind that you read about in the paper: kids starved to a scary forty-five pounds, made to drink ammonia, or attacked with tire irons. Q was not psychotic. He did have a temper. A lot of kids are pushed around. I'd have more grounds against my mom. Her abuse, if indeed it could be classified as that, was neglect. Mom was just as casual and distant as a deity.

Soon, I heard Mom in the kitchen. She was cooking. She never called me in.

My mother never let me touch her face. Even when I was little. Whenever I tried, she pushed my hands away. After a while, I stopped trying.

Outside, church bells rang. It was eight o'clock. Only eight o'clock. I wasn't tired, and I was all out of cigarettes. I could hear the TV, and every now and then Q's laughter. He was watching *Heroes*. He was a big fan of the cheerleader.

I went into my knapsack, digging for a stray cig, and pulled out that book Mr. Brook had given me.

Before I opened it, I looked at the cover and the yellowing pages. He must have had it forever. The cover price said sixty cents.

The opening page had a plate reading:

Please return this book to
Jerome Halbrook
1830 Rittenhouse Square, Apt. 5B
Philadelphia, PA 19130

What, did he expect someone to drop it off on his doorstep? Or like someone would actually pay the postage and drop it in a mailbox for him? Ha. He was so old-fashioned.

Then I thought some more. He gave me a book with his address in it. That was sly.

I looked at the lines and the marked and dog-eared pages. Some of the pages were warped, like he had been reading parts of it in the bathtub.

I opened the book to a random page: "To the Virgins, to Make Much of Time."

I threw the book across the room.

six

Mr. Brook, who was now subbing in Mrs. Simpson's English class, looked up from the attendance sheet as I busted into the room. I placed the *Immortal Poetry* before him, saying, "I finished it."

"All of it?" he asked skeptically.

"Yep."

"How was it?"

"Good."

There was a silence, then he questioned, "Are you all right?"

"I'm fine," I answered, and began walking away.

"Samara," he called. "It's not fast food. It's not meant to be consumed so quickly."

I turned to him. "And how do you know how fast I eat a Big Mac?"

He held the book out for me. "This is meant to be savored. Lingered over. Borrow it again."

I took out a cigarette and placed his book in my knapsack.

He smiled. "And don't smoke!"

When I got home, I thought I had entered some cheap-romance-novel parallel universe. I peered through the window only to see a two-hundred-fifty-pound woman in a thong and Q with his arms all over her. I blinked a few times just to make sure this wasn't some kind of illusion. But each time I did, the woman looked just as tawdry, and Q, who was in his customary undershirt and baggy jeans, seemed just as grabby. I couldn't tell if this was just the beginning or it had been raging all afternoon. I was only a few minutes early, taking, for a change, a quick pace rather than moseying home as usual.

Well, I'll be a monkey's uncle, I thought. Q had all the nerve in the world. My mother was at work just twelve blocks away, supporting his lazy butt, and he was turning this house further into his playground.

I ducked down under the windowsill so they couldn't see that I'd spotted them. I breathed some air and craved a cigarette but suppressed that urge. An idea had come to me.

I crept away, looking over my shoulder to avoid detection. At the end of the block, I stood up and started running with abandon. I didn't stop until I was right up on the main entrance of the hospital where my mother worked. As I took the elevator to the fifth floor, my heart pounded from the trip, the anticipation, and the secret I planned to spill.

My mom and a group of other women in blue smocks stood in a cluster at the nurses' station, laughing and slapping each other on the shoulders. I broke up their fun. My mother's eyes went fast to me. Her color rose. She left the crowd without saying a word of goodbye to them. She grabbed me by my arm and led me to the stairwell, which was made of cement and had a bright yellow railing and smelled like a musty cloakroom.

"What are you doing here?" she asked.

"I have news for you—" Since she didn't mince words, why should I? I was just about to tell her that Q screwed around on her, but she cut me off.

"You came down here interrupting my work."

I rolled my eyes. "Yeah, you're real busy."

Her long limp hands went to her side pocket to get a cigarette. She began to smoke. "I am at work." Her voice seemed to bounce in this dark stairway. "What do you want? And don't tell me you got into it with Q again. Why can't you give him some space? I'm not going to listen to this time and time again, Samara. You don't like him, go live somewhere else."

My mouth opened but no words came out. Over the past fifteen years she had told me this same thing fifteen thousand times. Message received: I was part of her present, but I had no bearing on her future. When I was gone, there would be more money to spend on her nails and her hair. I was sure the champagne corks would pop on the day of my departure. When she was old and gray, she wouldn't hit me up for aid. She would wheel her own self into a nursing home.

"Why can't he live somewhere else?" I finally asked. My body stiffened as if anticipating a blow. She wasn't a hitter, though. I knew this. She was a bitter.

"You're a grown woman, practically. You're nearly sixteen years old. I'm supposed to give up what I have for you? Then where will I be? I'm not going to be without someone in my life."

"And that's all that's important."

"Don't you listen?" she said quickly. (Couldn't she have hesitated just a little?) "I gave up a lot when I had you. I could have been free. I've always given to you. You just don't want to admit it." She stopped venting only long enough to take a deep drag.

I censored any retort I was thinking of and retreated, as I always did. I decided not to tell her about the strange woman I had seen at our house and what Q was doing with her.

I clenched the dark words inside me.

Let her think her man was faithful; that was somehow crueler.

A few moments later, the sunlight licked my face. At my feet four blocks from the hospital, there were fast-food wrappers, loose milk crates, and pee-stained mattresses. I ambled through Philly like I was homeless. Then it struck me: *like I was homeless?* What did I have to go home to?

I walked, counting the cracks of the sidewalk. It was only a little after four. I wasn't headed anywhere; I was just murdering time. In this post-dressing-down-from-my-mother daze, I found myself near Sixteenth. I stood frozen in a Gap storefront, and time leaped to a little after five. Car horns beeped, high heels clicked, and suitcases rolled. People had cell phone conversations of which I was privy to only one side.

An idea popped into my mind: Mr. Brook. He was only a few streets away. He'd be home right now. Though I had his address committed to memory, I patted the spot in my knapsack where the book *Immortal Poetry* rested. I had been carrying it around like a rabbit's foot.

The sun came through the buildings.

I wished it was night. I liked the moon better. She wasn't as cloying.

She was always alone; she didn't seem to mind.

She was awake when most people were asleep and vice versa.

She did her own thing.

Why did I suddenly feel the need to need someone? Why couldn't I continue to exist solo? I was certain that I was the only fifteen-year-old in the world who had a crush on her senior-citizen substitute teacher. In solitude, I stood outside his building, wondering what it was like inside. I bet there were full bookshelves along the walls of the living room, and photos in wooden frames.

A man came up behind me. He was a small man with a very long chin. Trusting and friendly, he held the front door for me. It would be so easy to get in.

I shook my head.

My eyes turned to what I thought was Mr.

Brook's window. I wondered—just what was he doing in there? Finishing his preparation of dinner? He was so neat, I bet he wore an apron.

Or was he a takeout kind of a guy? (I saw those delivery cyclists all over this part of town.)

Either way, there would be starched linen cloth with patterned borders. There would be a tumbler full of teaspoons and a silver cream pitcher and a china sugar bowl. (Even rich, rich people don't use china every day, do they?)

It was almost six now. Maybe he would be on dessert already. I could see it. It would be a chocolate something—something decadent, calorie laden, and gooey.

There would be a little mango slice on top.

Oh, Mr. Brook, you are so much better than orangutans or cigarettes.

The heavens seemed to roar as I stood outside his door, sighing. I felt alive.

Right then I made up my mind. I wasn't going to fasten myself to the railway line or throw myself off a bridge: I was going to seduce my sub.

I turned to walk home. By the next block, my hands were getting cold. Of course, I didn't have any gear, and the jacket I had on didn't have pockets, so I stretched my sleeves over my hands.

"Nice gloves," a stranger said to me.

seven

In homeroom, I received a summons. Grudgingly, I got up and made my way to the guidance counselor's office.

I shook the note at Bowman. "What's this about? I'm coming to school now."

He twittered, "This is not about that."

"Well, what is it about?"

He let out a long sigh. And his beady eyes went wide with pity. "Is everything all right . . . at home?"

"You're kidding me, right?" I asked. It was as if April Fools' had come in October.

"Please sit down. There's nothing to be ashamed of," Bowman continued.

I remained standing. "Why are you asking me?"

"I've gotten a report."

"A report?"

"Yes, a report." He was speaking to me so calmly, so gently, it was freaking me out. Whenever someone speaks like that, get ready for free-fall mode. Check the ground underneath your feet; it just might be shifting.

"From who?" I asked.

"That's not important. What is important is—" he began.

That was when I bolted.

"Samara! Samara!" His voice thickened as he called after me.

I scaled the stairs and when I reached the middle of the floor, I stormed into the substitute's room. He was alone, writing something on the board.

"What did you tell Bowman?" I asked him.

"Nothing specific. I just had a hunch about what might be going on and I thought it best to consult Mr. Bowman."

"And you didn't even think to give me a heads-up first? You didn't think to talk to me first? I mean, this is my life."

"He is a trained specialist, Samara."

"He's an idiot!" I burst out.

"He's a guidance counselor," Mr. Brook insisted.

"He's useless. Do you know how many times I've been to his office? I'm on frequent-flyer miles."

"Have you ever opened up to him?" Mr. Brook asked.

"No, I never have, and that's the way I plan to keep it," I told him plaintively.

I read his blue eyes, which were narrowing with pity for me.

"Oh, you're so nice," I spat out. "You are so concerned. If you wanted to know, why didn't you ask? Don't pawn me off to some amateur shrink."

This was the closest I'd ever been to him. My heart beat fast. I moved even closer.

Mr. Brook knew what I was doing and stepped back.

"Don't tell me you've never thought of it!" I said.

"What?"

"This." I went at him with my lips.

He pushed me away by the shoulders.

"I haven't," he told me.

I smirked, still not on to things. "Liar. You could have just said hi and bye. You saw me in that bookstore. We went to lunch. You've been sending me signals since the moment you laid eyes on me. I can read between the lines."

"I do like you—"

"Exactly."

"—but you're fifteen. I'm five times your age."

"I'm as old as you want me to be, Mr. Brook." I leaned close to him again.

He dodged me. "Samara, you should be interested in someone your own age."

Now I looked away and lowered my head. There was a joke to all of this, and there I was: the punch line.

"There are no interesting guys my own age. You act like you're handing me back my innocence. I don't have any, Mr. Brook. This is the new millennium. Post-9/11. Post–R. Kelly. I love you, with all my heart."

"Then your heart is confused."

"You think my heart is confused now! Before you, I was in love with an orangutan!" I screamed. Feeling my skin on fire, I ran out of the room.

eight

I reflected: my first and last try as a seductress had gone all wrong. My life was awful again.

I ducked out a side door and evaded school security to mix into the general public. I walked, or rather swam. It was raining hard, and I became one more unhappy fish in this city's aquarium of life.

I felt the rain on my bare head and through my sneaks, which leaked. My drab-colored shirt and my jeans went slick-bright with this wet, and I felt a strange boost. I was through the looking-glass, down was up, up down.

I lit a smoke.

* * *

When I got home, I expected to see Q with his supersized mistress, but that day Q's only companion was that *Texas Justice* judge and the smell of fried beef and popcorn (Q's late lunch?). I walked behind the couch, nearly tripping on a Pringles can. (What an oddity, the way they package those potato chips. It's like they really wanted to make tennis balls.)

I marched to my pathetic room still wringing wet. The walls' ugly paneling was showing its age. The wood was splitting. The rug was worn in spots, especially at the opening of the closet. I searched for some dry clothes.

I took off my soaked jeans and top and threw them in the hamper, which was overflowing.

I changed and still felt miserable.

As the afternoon wore on, I decided to make myself some dinner, but the fridge was a nightmare of rotting, spilling, stinking messes. Q had a habit of sticking anything in it, any way he wanted. There was a plate of unpopped popcorn kernels, and stale greening bread in loose plastic, and half a lemon meringue pie with a napkin draped over the top of it. There were five jars of peanut butter, two of which were empty. I swished the milk carton only to find its contents had turned to yogurt. I closed the door in disgust. I tried the cupboard on the back porch and pulled the string for the light. The bad bulb flickered, struggling to live. Going. Going. Gone.

I pulled the string again and the string broke.

Then and there, I decided to call it a day.

nine

A few days later, when I didn't see Flanders first period, my heart began to pound, pound, pound. I feared the worst and wouldn't you know it: the worst walked in.

I must be on God's hit list. Why else would he torture me like this?

Mr. Brook strolled in all purposeful and sharp.

A few people clapped.

Steph'Annie elbowed me.

Mr. Brook explained that Flanders would be taking the next couple of weeks off, due to her recurring rash. He went into the introduction business, as if any of us could forget he was Mr. Jerome Halbrook. That voice. That carriage. That handsome face with the aquiline nose. He was so distinguished. Mr. Brook had straight, thin lips, too, which made me think even more of some sort of English nobility. But his best feature was that skin. It had such deep brown dignity. Despite my resistance, I was still into him.

He went on about someone named Emily Dickinson. He told us that back in the mid-nineteenth century the Civil War broke out, Lincoln was shot, and Edison invented the lightbulb, but Dickinson left her Amherst, Massachusetts, house only twice in thirty years. She never got married or had any kids. She used all her time to write more than a thousand poems.

"I would like to share her with you," he said.

He ran through some of her titles, "Because I Could Not Stop for Death," "I Felt a Funeral in My Brain," "I Like a Look of Agony," and "I Heard a Fly Buzz When I Died."

Death, funeral, agony, and more death. I rolled my eyes. I bet Dickinson was a lot of fun to be around.

As if reading my mind, Mr. Brook told us next

that Miss Dickinson often stayed in her room all day, choosing to write letters rather than brave face-to-face communication.

"How did she feel about e-mail?" someone in the second row asked.

"She went through her whole life, and she never fell in love with anyone?" someone in the third row asked.

"There are rumors," Mr. Brook told us. I couldn't help perking up.

"Rumors that she might have had a forbidden love," Mr. Brook said.

The class oohed and aahed.

"Some say she was helplessly in love with a married man named Thomas Wentworth Higginson. He was a major literary critic of the time. Others say she was a lesbian."

"A lesbian? You mean like with women?" the AP wannabe asked.

Steph'Annie rolled her eyes and told Mr. Brook, "He was absent that day in health class."

"I've never heard that Emily Dickinson was a lesbian," the AP wannabe insisted.

"This is all speculation. No one will ever know for sure."

"What do you believe, Mr. Halbrook?" Steph'Annie asked.

"I believe she was in love with the greatest love of all: herself."

The class really laughed at that.

Mr. Brook held up his hand to calm us and said,

" 'The Soul selects her own Society— / Then— shuts the Door.' She did what she wanted when she wanted."

While he passed out a sheet of paper he told us that in some countries poets were persecuted. "In Russia, Stalin targeted artists during the Great Purge and shipped them off to labor camps. In America, poets have it even harder. Here, we ignore them. . . . Who would like to read this for us?"

There were twenty-eight other people in that English class. I felt sure he wouldn't call on me, but I avoided his eyes all the same.

"Samara will," Steph'Annie called out.

I sank down farther in my seat.

Mr. Brook looked at me a long time, and his eyes

shone. "It seems you've been volunteered. May I trouble you?"

So he did it. What nerve! A new weakness overtook me, then an expanding anger. Why didn't he just tie a rock around my neck and drown me in the Schuylkill River?

"Samara," he repeated, "would you please read for us?"

Steph'Annie peered at me with big, anxious eyes. Other necks were swiveled toward me.

Enough of this shameful cowardice! I thought. *All right, Mr. Brook, you're the boss.* I took the sheet of paper in my hands and held it at a proper distance.

I began reading good ole number 341. "After Great Pain, a Formal Feeling Comes." I comprehended each word of Dickinson's keen, melancholy verse. The last two lines brought the meaning home. "As Freezing persons recollect the Snow— / First—Chill—then Stupor—then the letting go."

I returned the paper to my desk and looked directly into the blue eyes and black face of Mr. Brook. Dickinson was right; we do tend to cling to things, like trees cling to the last of their leaves.

"Thank you, Samara," he said.

"No," I said. "Thank you."

More oohs and aahs from the class.

The bell rang. I, like the rest of the class, bustled out the door with a sharp right into the hall. I could hear Steph'Annie say my name behind me, but I didn't slow down. I made it to Rosetti's Algebra II, which was two flights up, in one minute, thirty-five seconds. That had to be some kind of Olympic record. My customary seat was three rows down, and I again ducked deep into obscurity.

I detested this class. Mr. Rosetti flipped when anyone got the wrong answer. He'd explode, telling us how wrong answers inflamed his hot Italian temper.

Is it politically incorrect when you're insulting yourself?

Mr. Rosetti also had an unfortunate shape. All his extra weight went directly to his abdomen. My teacher for the next period, Mr. Scafonas, had exactly the same body type. He had a normal head, legs, and arms. All his weight centered in his torso. Mr. Scafonas, however, was more jovial, I guess because there were more jokes to be made about psych. That day, he lectured on anomie, a state of anarchy, not to be confused with that Japanese form of animation.

Ha, ha. You see, I was over Mr. Brook. Way over him. I could laugh. My mind was clear. I had completely let go.

Of course, Steph'Annie didn't know that. Before fourth period, she caught me by my locker and tried her best to keep the pot churned.

"Boy, that sub really digs you. I felt it in the air. The electricity."

I frowned. "Then it must be about to storm."

"You are so cool in front of him. You don't let on at all."

"There's nothing to let on, Steph'Annie."

"Oh, I could listen to you two read all day. Tell me when you're going to burn your first CD. It'll be better than Jack Kerouac."

"Who?"

"He was a beatnik."

"A whatnik?" I asked.

"You know what I'm talking about." She smiled

her blue painted smile. "You know, those people in the cafés who played the bongos."

"I'm not with them, Steph'Annie," I said, closing my locker. "I don't even own a beret."

"You're always cutting yourself down. You are way cool. You have to come hang out with me this Friday."

"This Friday?" I asked.

"Yes, are you busy?"

"No," I said. I didn't have to think about it. I was never busy.

"Then come hang out." Her blue hair gleamed.

I found myself saying, "Sure."

ten

At night, South Street always had a thriving crowd. Most people were heavily tattooed with snakes and birds and circles and squares. The heavily-pierced-and-estranged were huddled in the alleyways with signs. Most of them were male. I have heard a theory that many homeless kids are gay, and that their parents have tossed them out, choosing to have no child rather than a gay one.

I looked at them with a kind of hunger, a need to know what had been the tipping point.

Had they been thrown out headfirst, or had they maintained some dignity in the matter and left of their own accord?

The wind whirled like crazy. I read their sloppily scripted signs: HOMELESS, HUNGRY, FAR FROM HOME. PLEASE GIVE MONEY. WHATEVER YOU CAN. . . .

I wondered, did they ever look back? Long for living indoors and having three square meals a day? Did they miss it enough to beg back in?

I spotted Steph'Annie and her friends on the corner of Seventh and South. Steph'Annie had on her customary gear. Her pals, however, were dressed maddeningly ordinarily, almost Beyoncé style. Their coats were open, revealing low-rider jeans and half tops. Instead of blue, both of them had red lipstick on.

Steph'Annie introduced Roxanne and Kath. Roxanne had a long narrow face and a long narrow frame. She kept her somewhat large nose pointed at her cell phone as she frantically text-messaged her ex-boyfriend—ex as of two days ago, that is. The body wasn't even cold. She said a "Hi, Samara" with a slight lisp, then went back to texting.

I could only wish that the other girl shared her penchant for brevity. The other girl, Kath, was small but chesty. Faster than the speed of light, her lips moved. Her voice sounded high and squeaky.

"So where are we going? What are we eating?" she asked. "I hope not pizza. I had pizza for lunch. Not the round kind, the square. Is the square kind still considered pizza?"

I knew I shouldn't make snap judgments. But I couldn't help thinking it was going to be a loooooooooong night.

Steph'Annie planned for us to go to the Rocket. She promised it would be just like that old seventies TV show about the fifties. I expected the waitresses to have poodle skirts and swishy ponytails, but I had no idea what the men wore during that time period.

Inside, the jukebox played a tune called "Trickle Trickle." As far as I could tell, the song was about rain and a boy who wanted to kiss a girl. But we hadn't come for the doo-wop. We'd come to get our arteries clogged with whole-milk milk shakes and one-hundred-percent-pure-beef burgers, heavy on the onions.

We sat in the booth for a while before anyone waited on us.

Finally a young man came in. He unfolded his apron and carefully put it around his waist; then he neatly fit his cap over his dreadlocks. I figured it must be some sort of shift change because he came right over and distributed four glasses of ice water and four jumbo-sized menus.

I knew him from somewhere. It wasn't school, I was sure of that. It was strange; he was like someone I had seen in a movie. That face, that slight frame. But what sense did that make, a movie star waiting tables?

While the rest of us perused the menu, Steph'Annie announced that she'd have a burger.

"I thought you were going veg?" Kath asked.

Steph'Annie smiled. "It's Friday. I'm only veg on weekdays."

"Friday's not a weekday?" Kath persisted in her tiny, squeaky voice.

I looked over at Roxanne, who was text-messaging so frantically she looked like she was defusing a bomb. Instead of fiddling with the red wire, blue wire, she was punching those assorted keys till her fingers burned. I felt like I was watching an episode of *24*.

She held a message out for us to read. Her ex had written, "I'm at Burger King."

"So, we're here," Steph'Annie said. "Tell him to get lost."

The waiter came back to take our order.

Kath began. "I'll have a sweet roll and coffee and a milk shake."

The waiter nodded.

"Aren't you going to write that down?" Kath asked him. "You know what they say—the weakest pen is better than the strongest memory."

"I think he knows his job!" I said, hoping my words didn't make me sound as fed up as I really was. I would never know, because the waiter snapped his finger and pointed at me. "The zoo. I remember you from the zoo."

Kath laughed loudly.

"It was a few weeks ago. Remember?" he asked.

It all came together. Of course, I nodded. This was that weirdo who tried to get Dru into a fit.

"I'm Jeff." He held out his hand.

I shook it quickly. He gave me a long, searching look.

I caught my breath. "I'll have a Coke and a burger, well done."

Steph'Annie ducked her head between us. "I don't mean to interrupt, but I'll have what she's having."

Roxanne looked up from her phone quickly to say, "Ditto. And with cheese."

He collected our menus. "Coming right up," he said, and walked back to the kitchen.

"He likes you!" Steph'Annie exclaimed as she gripped my knee. "Did you see the way he looked at you?"

"What a spaz," Kath said.

"He's cute," Roxanne said, looking up from her cell momentarily.

"He's a cute spaz," Steph'Annie said.

"He seems like a geek," Kath said. "I bet he listens to Clay Aiken."

I glanced his way and watched him fill the sugar

bowls. Sure, he had soulful eyes and an easy smile, but who was into that?

He jogged over to our table and asked me, "Did you want something?"

"Samara wants to give you her phone number," Steph'Annie told him.

"She does?" I asked.

"Samara. That's a pretty name," he said. "I'm Jeff."

"You told her that," Kath said.

Steph'Annie dug in her purple pocketbook and revealed a slip of paper and a pen.

Jeff took them and started writing. "Here's mine," he said. A bell rang and he was off again.

"What is he doing working here? I don't think they had dreadlocks in the fifties," Kath said matter-of-factly.

"Maybe they did—in Jamaica," Steph'Annie said.

"I heard that seventy different species of insects live in hair like that."

"What?" Steph'Annie and I asked.

"Microscopic bugs. Seventy of them," Kath repeated.

"I'm sure he doesn't have bugs in his hair," I said. I was beyond the point of hating her. Her voice was like a knife scratching on glass to me.

"How does he wash it?" Kath asked.

"Everybody washes their hair, Kath," Steph'Annie told her.

"Yeah, but how?" she asked with a flick of her store-bought ponytail.

When our plates came, Kath offered me some of her sweet roll.

"No, thank you," I said with a phony smile.

Roxanne took a bite of her condiment-laden hamburger and the ketchup dripped onto her cell phone.

I turned to Steph'Annie. "What am I going to do with his phone number?"

She took one more bite of her burger, then answered. "The way I see it, you have two options. You could either call him or you could call him."

I nodded. "I see I have a lot of options."

"That's what friends are for," Steph'Annie said. She seemed so satisfied with herself. I should have known she liked meddling and matchmaking.

I glanced over at Jeff, and he winked at me.

"Oh my God, did you see that!" Steph'Annie yelped.

"Are you going to date him?" Kath asked me.

"I don't know," I mumbled.

"You don't know?" Steph punched my arm.

Kath frowned. "Dammit, now we have to leave a tip."

eleven

"Kath and Roxanne think you're way cool!" Steph'Annie told me the next day.

Really? I couldn't stand either one of them, I thought. Steph'Annie and I walked along the cobblestone walkways of Old City. It didn't take long to get on the topic of Mr. Brook. All roads led to him. I told her how I had run into him in the bookstore.

"I really ought to start reading. I mean really reading—get away from the magazine rack, you know? . . . I don't think they really want people to buy books anymore. It's all chai and DVDs. . . . That is one hot old dude, and he took you to lunch."

"We *had* lunch—it's not like he asked me out. It was a chance encounter."

"Yeah, but you got there. He likes you," she squealed. "He is so handsome. He's superhandsome. He's like Denzel Washington and Richard Gere handsome—they're in their seventies, right?"

I shrugged. I really didn't follow heartthrobs. Why should I care about all the ins and outs of those celebs? Did they care about my goings-on?

We were headed uptown toward where Mr. Brook lived.

"You know where he lives. He took you to his pad."

"I never went to his pad. I just stood outside it."

"That is so cool. You had a vigil. You have to show me where he lives."

Next thing I knew, we were camped outside his apartment.

She asked for my lighter, and when I gave it to her, she flicked it and held it up and swayed.

"This is what they do at concerts."

Amused passersby looked at us.

"Wow! He lives here, Samara. He's rich and he's a substitute teacher. . . . Let's drop in."

"No!" I screamed.

"I'll call to him. Hello! I say there, Mr. Jerome Halbrook, hello there!" Steph'Annie affected a British accent as she called up to him.

"Steph'Annie!"

"Okay. Okay. I'll stop."

We walked away from the building.

Steph'Annie pinched my arm. "Have you called dude yet?"

"Dude?" I asked.

"Dude, from the fifties joint."

"No."

She screeched and said, "Somebody knows the rules."

"I just don't want to throw myself at him."

Steph'Annie snapped her fingers. "Talk that talk, man trap. So you'll call him tonight?"

"Isn't the guy supposed to be the one who initiates things?"

"You must think you're in one of those poems

that sub brought in. It's the twenty-first century. It's okay for you to pursue him. Besides, you know he's interested."

"I don't know for a fact. Anyway, I don't want to look like I have nothing going on."

"What *do* you have going on?"

"Nothing. But I have my pride."

"Swallow your pride. Dial the ten digits. Don't be coy."

I wasn't used to being nice and trying to make friends. But I ended up calling him. Trying to, without the aid of that self-help book I kept meaning to read.

"Hello . . . Jeff?" I said haltingly.

"Samara?" he asked in a shaky, thin voice. He sounded as nervous as I was, but that of course didn't affect my timidness.

I wanted a cigarette badly, but I forged ahead without the vice. At the end of our talk, he asked me on a date.

I said yes.

twelve

Everything was set for my first-ever-in-my-whole-life date. It was to be Friday at six. I spent the time leading up to it hoping the night would be a failure. Because Jeff was hot, I didn't want it to work out. Dating him would be like eating ice cream; it would just be a matter of time before it disappeared. Everything taps out, and then what would I be left with? Sweet memories? Sticky fingers? Solitude again? If I liked to write, I thought I would make a wonderful Emily Dickinson. Who needs human contact, anyway?

Mr. Brook was back on Monday. Like a pint of Häagen-Dazs Rocky Road, he stood there taunting me. At room temperature, I was the one that melted.

"May I see you for a minute after class?" he asked.

"I don't have a minute after class; I have to get to algebra," I told him, hoping to sound strong.

"Well then." Unflustered, he grinned. "Whenever you can squeeze me in."

Who was I kidding? Just seeing him filled my heart with joy. I quavered, though—why did he want to see me? I began to worry that he'd seen Steph'Annie and me goofing around outside his apartment. I thought a little more and guessed maybe it was about the last time we'd spoken when I had exploded in anger. By lunch, I couldn't hold back any longer. I found him in his empty classroom perusing the *New York Times*.

"Look, I'm sorry I spoke to you the way I did last week. I didn't mean any of it. I know you were only trying to help."

"You don't have to—"

"Oh, yes, I do. I want to clear the air."

"The air is pretty clear, Samara."

"Right. Sure. That's why you asked me to see you."

"That's not why I asked to see you."

"Then why?"

"Have you finished the book?"

"Book? You mean *Immortal Poetry*?"

"Yes."

I lied. "I read a little of it."

"Good. I'm glad you're savoring it," he said, then returned to his *New York Times*.

"That's it?" I asked.

He peered at the arts section. "Yes."

"That's all you wanted to ask me?" I asked. Again.

He nodded. "Yes."

"It's just a stupid book. Why do you care so much?"

He folded the paper. "I care for you, Samara."

"Then why did you push me away last week?"

"Because I care for you."

Angry and exasperated, I decided to storm out, but before I did, I wanted to tell him one more thing. "You know what you are?" I asked him. "You are a needle."

"A needle can either mend or pierce," he told me.

"Well, you're definitely not stitching."

"Let me try a new thread."

I turned to leave. "Save your thread."

"Samara—"

"Don't."

"Don't what?"

"Whatever . . . Let's just stop it. I mean, there's not anything between you and me, and there shouldn't be, so let's just stop it. Everything."

I was at the door, seconds away from my exit.

"Page one eighty-two," he said.

"Huh?"

"One-eight-two. In the book. I want you to read that poem, when you can. . . . No rush."

Now I really, really, really wanted to leave.

"Samara."

"What?"

"I remember being your age. I was confused and lonely and no one understood me. I'm from the South, and there boys were supposed to play football and be interested in cars and I always went to the library. I liked to read. I remember looking at a map of the world. You know, those big ones that fold out. I stared at it seemingly for hours. Who do I want to be? Where do I want to go?"

"You did all that studying, and you still ended up in Philadelphia."

He smiled. "I walked right into that one, didn't I? All I'm saying is that if you let your dreams die, life becomes monotonous. Life becomes just one long string of Mondays and Tuesdays and Wednesdays and—"

"I know the days of the week." I interrupted him.

"Life becomes bleak with despair if you let it. . . . I hope you reported him to the proper authorities."

I recoiled. "Who?"

"That man who was inappropriate to you."

My whole body went cold. "How could you possibly—"

"The way you reacted to that first poem I brought in."

I didn't know what to say. Was that why he

sicced Bowman on me? How could he know from one answer what my mother *still* didn't believe? "He used to come into my room. Most of the time he'd just feel me up and kiss on me, but sometimes . . ." I trailed off.

"How old were you?"

"Eleven."

"Didn't you tell your mother?"

"She was hard to get to. She thought she'd hit the jackpot with him. He was an engineer. I don't know what engineers do, but I know that's a good job and he made a lot of money. He fixed a lot of things around the house."

"Samara—" he began, but I kept on talking over his words.

"I got lucky, though. His great job ended up saving me. He got transferred to California," I said in one breath before exiting. I went to the girls' room to splash some cool water on my face. It was burning.

thirteen

Their low voices broke off when I entered.

Q and Q's mistress (she had on a different wig; it fit like a thick black hood around her face) turned just in time to catch me ducking into my room. I quickly busied myself. I flicked on the radio and turned the dial from easy listening to Top 40 to salsa. This station blared trumpets, trombones, maracas, and congas. It matched the fury of Q when he busted in.

"What are you doing?" he yelled.

I sat at the edge of my bed. *Remain cool*, I told myself.

"What are you going to do?" he continued.

"Your secret's safe with me," I mumbled.

He approached me, drawing closer until his breath was on me. It smelled like a mixture of Funyuns and Mountain Dew.

"It better be," he said; then he slammed the door when he left.

I lay down on the bed. I remembered the hospital, how Mom had cut me down before I could mount my protest.

Mr. Brook was right. You have to make your own tomorrow. But how?

I hated my home, but I couldn't imagine doing what he did—going to a library one afternoon and sitting at one of those big tables, pulling out one of those huge maps and looking at it, studying it, circling which places I'd like to visit.

Where do I want to live?

What country of bliss?

What is the zip code for happiness?

The next day in class, there was a great frenzy up front. Kids were pointing to the floor, saying, "Look at them!"

"What are you referring to?" Mr. Brook asked.

"There's a trail of ants!" the AP wannabe screeched.

"Well, they want to learn, too," Mr. Brook quipped. "Just because they aren't enrolled doesn't mean they can't sit in."

The class laughed as they moved purses, lunch bags, and knapsacks off the floor. Some even drew their legs up on their chairs. Mr. Brook was unfreaked by the goings-on. He was such a change from Flanders. I remembered once there was a fire drill, and she was the first one out of the classroom, shoving the girl who sat by the door out of her way.

Then again, what did Mr. Brooks have to fear? Those ants wouldn't dare try to get up his pants legs or over his leather shoes.

He was reading Langston Hughes with such looseness, especially the last few lines: "So since I'm still here livin', / I guess I will live on. / I could've died for love— / But for livin' I was born."

"You can really rock the mike," Steph'Annie said as she stood and started her own standing ovation. "That was like, whoa!"

He explained that this Langston Hughes was born in Joplin, Missouri, but went on to become the most important writer of something that was referred to as the Harlem Renaissance, which was a blossoming of blacks in the arts. Hughes traveled to West Africa in the 1920s, the U.S.S.R. in the 1930s, and Korea in the 1940s.

"He must have been rich," said the girl in front who was afraid of ants.

"Was he in the army?" someone else asked.

"Actually, he worked his way across the world as a ship steward."

"He took a boat?" the AP wannabe asked.

"That's the best way to go. Out there in the big blue. How many of you have ever been at sea?" Mr. Brook asked.

A boy in a muscle shirt waved him away. "Man, that's too much water."

"Yeah, we don't even like to get in the bathtub," someone up front called out.

Mr. Brook got back on topic, telling us Langston Hughes wrote sixteen volumes of poems, three short-story collections, two novels, twenty plays, and more—and I thought Emily Dickinson had too much time on her hands.

"Langston Hughes said that poetry should be direct, comprehensible, and the epitome of simplicity," Mr. Brook told us.

"What does 'epitome' mean?" asked the girl who was afraid of ants.

I popped in on him during his free period, saying, "Leave it to you to cheer us up with a suicide poem."

"Samara," he said happily.

"That was the best one yet," I said, stepping into the room.

"I thought you would have recognized that poem. It was in the book I lent you, on page one eighty-two."

I gulped. "You caught me there. I'll read it tonight. I promise. I mean I really promise this time." I walked closer to him so I could get the full benefit of those blue eyes.

"Let's go to Ahab's again," I suggested. "We could catch up."

"I have somewhere to go after the workday," he told me.

"Oh," I said, and wondered if he could tell how fast my heart was sinking.

"I would like to go," he reassured me.

"But you have something more important," I said, then immediately felt like smacking myself.

"It's not like that, Samara."

"I didn't mean it like that," I said quickly. "So where do you have to go?"

"I can't say."

"Is it a secret?" I asked.

"I guess you could say that."

"If it's a secret, then you *have* to tell me."

He grinned. "I have a doctor's appointment."

"Well, then you better keep it. You old people should keep on top of things." I winked at him. As I headed for the door, I added, "I'm glad we're friends again."

"So am I, Samara," he said.

fourteen

That night I read *Immortal Poetry*, and into the next morning my head was swimming with images and ideas. On the school bus, for once I wasn't peering out the window expecting to see a man peeing on a tree. I was so gone. Oh, Mr. Brook, Mr. Brook, Mr. Brook.

As I entered my first-period class, I didn't see Mr. Brook with all his debonair allure. Bowman's bland countenance took his place. He told us he would be our substitute, and we should catch up on our studies for other classes.

"What happened to the old dude?" asked the AP wannabe.

"Just take something out and work on it," Bowman told him.

Steph'Annie's eyes were like saucers. She scribbled in the margin of her notebook, "Where do you think he is?"

I wrote back, "I'm going to find out."

I stood, inhaled deeply, threw back my shoulders, and approached Bowman. "Where is he?"

"He's not here," Bowman said. He had files spread out on the desk. He was making notations in them and didn't look up to answer.

"I can see that. Where is he?"

"Hahnemann University Hospital," he said finally.

"What!" I exclaimed.

Steph'Annie eyed me quizzically from the third row.

Bowman shifted his position but still didn't look at me.

He whispered this part. "Look, I don't know what's going on between you two, but his cancer—"

"His cancer? He doesn't have any cancer," I said loudly. "He's fine. I saw him just yesterday."

Now everyone was looking.

"That's the way cancer works, Samara. It doesn't hurt until it starts to hurt, and then it really hurts. He had lung cancer a few years back. It had been in remission but now it's spread to his brain."

"No. That can't be."

"It's causing bleeding, and they are trying to stabilize him. Now that's all I know, Samara." Bowman's eyes finally snapped to me. "Please return to your seat."

Instead, as if I were in a trance, I went into the hallway.

He followed me. "Where are you going?" he asked. "There's nothing you can do."

I ignored him and walked.

"Samara, come back here."

I ignored his calls and continued toward an exit. I'd never tried it like this, escaping in plain sight.

"Samara," Bowman bellowed from the doorway. "Get back in the classroom."

Steph'Annie came out, squeezing behind Bowman without detection. She mouthed to me to meet her in the girls' room.

"Samara, if you take one more step, I will call the police and have them deal with you."

I stopped walking. "Okay," I said. "Let me get myself together." I pointed to the restroom.

"I'll give you two minutes."

I nodded and kept nodding and feigning agreement.

"Two minutes." He held up two fingers.

I met up with Steph'Annie by the stalls; we ran down the back stairs and escaped into the world.

I hated the hospital. I hated the whole lame setup: there's never closure. First you have symptoms, then you wait; then you get the diagnosis, then you wait; more treatment, then you wait some more; then if you actually have something wrong, you get a lifetime of waiting.

I also hated Hahnemann because that was where Mom worked.

When we entered, Steph'Annie did most of the talking. "We're looking for Mr. Jerome Halbrook."

"Can you spell that?" the woman at the front

desk asked. She had a definite Philadelphia accent: nasal.

Steph'Annie took his name letter by letter and at the end told her, "We're his daughters."

After typing it into the computer, she told us, "He's in the intensive care unit."

"Damn" slipped out of my mouth. I was surprised I didn't say more.

"Where is that?" Steph'Annie asked.

"Right next to the emergency room."

"Shit," I said.

We hurried. The click of Steph'Annie's steel-toe boots was amplified in the bare halls.

At the entrance to the ICU, a heavily made-up nurse with bright red lips greeted us. "Who are you here to see?"

"Mr. Halbrook. We're his granddaughters," Steph'Annie said smoothly.

In intensive care, there were no doors, just curtains that you could quickly slide open for easy access. My worst fears were realized inside. In a crisp white-sheeted bed, Mr. Brook had breathing tubes

up his nose. He was on a monitor. Electronic equip-
ment up the wazoo, and he was out cold.

He's going to die, I thought.

Steph'Annie bowed, crossed herself, and told
me, "Maybe it's not as bad as it seems."

The curtain opened, and a mop-headed man
rushed in with a stethoscope around his neck and a
clipboard in hand.

"You're both his daughters?" he asked.

He was accompanied by that nurse with the
gardenia-red-painted lips from the hall and that
nasal-voiced attendant from the info booth.

"No, they're the granddaughters," the one from
the hall said skeptically.

The jig was up.

"No, actually, we're his nieces. And we have to
make a phone call to our other uncle," Steph'Annie
told them, clutching my hand as we made our way
to the curtain. "Come on, sis."

The regular cafeteria was closed. There was an al-
cove that had soft pink walls. All that was available

there was a bland assortment of things soft and sweet.

"Is this for the patients or us?" Steph'Annie pointed to the rice pudding.

I chose a lemon pie slice. She picked the pudding. We both got cocoa.

In this unpopulated space, we found a clean table and sat down.

"It's all a big conspiracy. The government has cures for everything, but it just doesn't want to use them. Health care is a billion-dollar industry." She took a sip of her beverage. "He'll be all right."

"He told me yesterday he had to go to the doctor. They must have taken him in then."

"He'll be all right, Samara. He was fine yesterday. People don't go downhill that quick."

"Did you just see what I did? Steph'Annie, he's in intensive care. That's the last exit on the turnpike."

"He's not going to die. He doesn't have the look."

"What look?"

"The look. Before my nana died, I knew it. I

could see it in her face. It was so washed out. Her features were gone. Plus, her legs were like sticks."

"When was this?" I asked.

"Last year. I was out of school for two weeks straight. Don't you remember? We had algebra together."

It didn't register. Last year? I didn't even know her name until just a few weeks ago. "I'm sorry about your grandmother."

"She wanted to die at home. She didn't want to be hooked up to anything. My mom okayed the ventilator anyway. Sometimes people come off that. It's just as well. She's in a better place."

"Better than SoSo?" I asked, not meaning it to come out as flippant as it sounded.

"You're a comedienne." She put a spoonful of her rice pudding into my cocoa.

Not counting it as a loss, I poured the cocoa into her rice pudding.

She took a scoop and flicked it on me. Luckily, I blinked before it hit my eye.

I searched for new ammo.

The pie was already running at room temperature.

Steph'Annie rose. She had a heart-shaped face. When she laughed, her tiny chin came to a sharp point. She backed away holding her hands out. "No. No. Please."

I crept toward her with that slice in my hand.

I aimed and fired.

It hit her square in the face.

"Samara!" I heard a scream. But it wasn't from Steph'Annie—she was picking the yellow glob out of her dyed blue hair.

I spun around and saw my mom.

fifteen

"What are you doing here again, Samara?" Mom demanded.

"I'm not here to see you," I told her.

Mom gestured at Steph'Annie. "Who's that? Who are you?"

"This is Steph'Annie."

"Hi, Mrs. Tuttle," Steph said.

"It's Miss," Mom quickly corrected her.

"There's a teacher who's—" I began.

"A teacher. What? What makes you think a teacher wants to see either of you?" Mom shot out her questions at bullet speed. There was no dodging them. "Steph'Annie what?"

"Huh?" Steph'Annie asked.

"What difference does it make?" I asked my mom.

"How long have you known her? Why does she dress like that?" Mom asked.

Steph'Annie scooped another hunk of pie off her face and held out her clean hand for Mom to shake. "It's Perdomo, Miss Tuttle."

Mom wouldn't shake her hand. She looked at her like she was contaminated. "How did you get a Spanish name?"

My face burned with embarrassment.

One of the blue smocks came up to Mom and told her she was needed on the floor.

"I want to talk to you when you get home," Mom told me before leaving.

The confrontation commenced as soon as I stepped in the door.

"Don't you ever do something like that again!" Mom told me.

"Like what?"

"You are supposed to be in school, for one thing."

"School? What difference does school make?"

"I don't see how you plan to lead a normal life—"

"Normal? Like what? Like you?"

"Samara, I saw you throw pie at that girl."

"We were just kidding around."

"In a hospital?"

"I know where I was."

"Why does she dress like that? And Perdomo, is that Spanish or Italian?"

"Sounds Eye-talian to me." Q rose to his feet. He just had to get into the act.

"What do you know, genius?" I asked him. "She's Afro Puerto Rican."

"I've never heard of that," he said.

"There's a lot of things you haven't heard of."

"You better watch it," he warned me.

"Why are you here, Q?"

"You don't have any say over anything," Q told me, pointing his finger in my face. "You need to learn to shut up."

I've been *shutting up,* I thought, *and where has it gotten me? I've been shutting up and taking shit from him for long enough*. I turned to my mother. "Let me tell you what's been going on here while you're at work."

He glared at me as he stepped closer to me. "I'm warning you."

Though he was so close I could feel his breath, I didn't retreat. I beamed at him. I wanted him to do something, and I wanted my mom to see it.

"Q's having a little trouble keeping it in his pants."

I enjoyed the momentary pleasure of watching the muscles in my mother's face quiver. She scrutinized me gravely for signs that I was lying. I gave her none. This was the most attention I had received from her since I could remember.

Q punched me before I could duck. I flew back and immediately tasted blood.

Holding my cheek, I turned my eyes to Mom.

"What are you going to do?" I asked her.

sixteen

The next morning the sky smelled like stale linen. Everything was fog. It was the kind of day when you wished it would snow, sleet, rain, or clear up already.

They were on to Steph'Annie and me as we approached the intensive care ward.

That cosmetic-junkie nurse headed us off at the pass.

"Immediate family only," she told us.

"Can't we even see him for a minute?" Steph'Annie asked.

"Immediate family only," she repeated, blocking the doorway that led to the intensive care unit.

"Is he up?" I asked.

"Immediate family," she said without inflection.

"You have been so helpful," Steph'Annie said.

She winked at us and said, "I take Christmas cards."

As we made our way back outside, Steph'Annie asked, "What happened to your face?"

I gave her the universal encrypted message for SOS. "I fell," I told her.

She nodded knowingly. "If you need a place to stay for a little while, I would love to have you stay over."

"I'll be all right. I'm sorry about yesterday. My mom acts like that."

"Don't be sorry. She's not the first person to think I'm weird. You sure you don't want to hide out?"

"I'll be all right."

She opened her arms wide for me and during her hug she said, "We'll come back later. It'll be a whole new crew."

We came back in the early evening only to be halted again.

It turned out that Mr. Jerome Halbrook had

left specific instructions that he didn't want to see anyone.

Steph'Annie squeezed my arm. "That's a good sign, Samara. At least he's up."

I came home dejected. The house was empty. It was Friday night. Q and Mom were out Red Lobstering it up. Having a real Olive Garden of a good time. Yippee!

I went to the kitchen and began microwaving a bag of popcorn. The phone rang. Whoever was on the other end was not giving up easily. It went ten times, then ceased. The microwave buzzer went off. Then the phone started ringing again. The microwave buzzer. Phone. Microwave. Phone.

I grabbed the bag and answered the phone.

"May I speak to Samara?" the voice asked.

"Jeff?" I asked. *That's right*, I thought, *I had a date tonight.*

"I'm sorry, I got an audition last minute, so I couldn't make it. I hope you didn't think you were being stood up. I tried calling you earlier, but some crazy man answered."

"That was no crazy man, that was my mother's boy toy," I said without thinking.

"He sounded young. Like our age. So you never got the message?"

"No, today's been a mess. I just got in—a friend of mine is in the hospital."

"Not the punk-looking one?" he asked.

"No. My sub."

"Your what?"

"This teacher who gave out poetry." I started choking up.

"What are you talking about?" he asked.

He was full of questions and the bag of popcorn was burning in my palm.

"Samara?"

"I'm sorry, Jeff. Can I call you back?"

He was saying something as I hung up on him.

My mother came in alone around ten that night. I was surprised she was Q-less. When I stepped into the kitchen, she was not so much cleaning as moving things around.

"How's your face?"

"What difference does it make?" I asked her.

"I asked you, didn't I?"

"How come you're never on my side? Besides being born, what have I ever done to you?"

She went back to moving a stack of papers from a chair to the top of the fridge. "Stay out of his way, Samara."

"You think really that's why I'm here, Mom? I don't mean in this house. I mean on this earth. Do you think I was put on this earth to get punched by your current boyfriend? Or to satisfy the lust of your former boyfriend?"

"I don't need this."

"So this one slaps me every now and then and the other one feels me up. What difference does it make?"

"You asked for that slap, Samara," she said bluntly.

"Sure I did. This is my fault. Everything is."

"By now you should have learned that if you stay out of a man's way he won't bother you."

"What do you think I've been trying to do? Of the parade of men that I have seen come through here, who have I started up with?"

"What do you want me to do, Samara?"

"*Something.* Put me first for a change. You gave that engineer full access."

"He said he never—"

"He was all over me, Ma."

"So you say, Samara."

"I'm telling you what happened. Why would I lie?"

"He's long gone, Samara. The time to tell me all this has passed."

"I told you then, Mom. You didn't do anything. If he didn't get transferred, he would still be after me. And now you let Q belt me one right in front of you. Do you expect me to stay here like a target?" I asked.

"You aren't the target, Samara—I am," she said in a hoarse and tired voice. "I'm an easy target. Everything that goes wrong is my fault. Your father walked before you were born. He never even tried to look after you, but I'm the bad one. I'm supposed to raise you alone, work, keep up a house without anyone's help. And God damn me if I ever want someone in my life to spend time with. When I do that, I'm selfish. Well, let me tell you something. I've done the best that I can, and when you get out there on the other side of that door you will find that you can't read minds and you don't know what's in everyone's heart and no one, no one is who you think they are. And maybe then you'll realize that I'm not the biggest monster going, Samara. I'm just your mother."

seventeen

So I didn't get along with my mother. Did that make me special? Out of the ordinary? It's not like I didn't try with her. All my life, I have been a chicken. A chicken scratching for seeds of concern in her soil.

If our fight had been a Movie of the Week, we would have found a way to iron things out if it had taken all night.

Maybe one day I'll write a memoir. Isn't that what everyone with a sucky childhood is supposed to do? Chronicle (and when possible, embellish) each and every slight till everything sounds really,

really, really bad. Then I'll get all the attention. All of it. Everyone will be talking about poor, pitiful Samara Tuttle.

In the following days, however, my mom and Q's problems took a serious backseat. Mr. Brook took center stage in my mind, even though I couldn't see him. I called the hospital every day instead, sometimes two or three times.

Mr. Brook was moved to the fourteenth floor, the rehab unit.

"Rehab?" I asked. "He doesn't drink."

"No. Physical rehabilitation," the person on the line repeated.

I waited ten minutes and phoned back to find out that a rehabilitation center is actually a good thing because it means you're close to dismissal. Another perk was that the rehab hospital has a wide-open-door policy. I could visit anytime.

So the next day, I played hooky. The fluorescent lights of the hospital hallway burned. I was going to see him, and I didn't care if his voice was a hoarse whisper or booming again. Or if his skin had gone from a proud dark brown to a timid light gray. Or if those brilliant blue eyes were shaded and withdrawn.

I was happy to see him looking as good as new. Mr. Brook was in blue slippers and a bathrobe. He was sitting in front of the tube.

The blaring TV reminded me of home, only Mr. Brook had on a game show.

Walking in, I felt that I was teetering off the edge of his flat earth. I placed a vase of flowers on the end table. Silence stretched as he held me in his grim straightforward stare.

The set was mounted on the wall too high to reach, so the remote control was essential. It was nestled in the palm of his hand.

Not daring to sit down, I shifted my weight from one leg to the other.

"I brought your book," I told him.

He said nothing.

"We're friends again, remember?" I said gently.

"I told them no visitors." I was taken aback by the testiness in his voice.

I fluffed his pillow.

More silence.

"Are you on some kind of drug?" I asked.

His face was fixed. "I'm not on any drugs; I refused them."

Was this Mr. Brook or had an invasion of the body snatchers taken place?

"This is no time to just say no. Your specialty is poetry, not medicine. I'm not sure you should be second-guessing medical professionals."

"If I'm meant to go, I'm meant to go."

"That's no way to talk."

"I will do what I want with the life I have left."

"The life you have left?" I asked. "You're in rehab. That means you're better."

"It just means your condition has stabilized, and they can't do anything else for you. You have to wait to die."

"Wait to what? Die?" I frantically cracked open *Immortal Poetry*.

"Close it," he ordered.

"You told me to—"

"Close it."

"But—"

"Do as I say."

I put the book down and started reciting from memory.

"But what about Dylan Thomas—'Do Not Go Gentle into That Good Night'? 'Old age should burn and rave at close of day; Rage, rage against the dying of the light.' "

He looked me straight in the eye and said, "Old MacDonald had a farm, e-i-e-i-o."

I drew back in horror.

"You're messing with my mind again," I told him. "You told me about hope and courage and making the most of things. Is that advice too good for you?"

"Samara, go to school. Do you know what time it is?"

"School?"

"I don't want you to take off school," he said.

"I don't want you to give up," I said.

"Don't come visit me anymore."

"Why?"

"I just told you."

He used his thumb to up the TV's volume. My heart beat violently. I heard: "MaryBeth Frazer. You are the next contestant on *The Price Is Right!*"

eighteen

I was like a trout swimming upstream. It was 11:17 a.m. on a Tuesday. I roamed the streets, thinking of all those contestants who jumped around like lunatics because they were told to "come on down." I had stayed with Mr. Brook until I couldn't stand it anymore.

That MaryBeth woman correctly guessed the cost of a Kenmore dishwasher, and now she had the chance to win a brand-new car!

I hated *The Price Is Right*! I hated anything that came between Mr. Brook and me—cancer, game shows, age gaps, teacher ethics . . . damn them all.

I would rather have seen him hooked up to a

million gadgets. His sophistication and warmth were replaced by frost and superficiality. My Mr. Brook watching daytime TV? My Mr. Brook would never be so easily entertained.

That night, I was haunted by my Mr. Brook. In my nightmare, I had an IV needle in my arm and there was a steady drip of "Get out! Get out! Get out!"

After Bowman's one-day fill-in, a parade of subs took stints: a weird guy with medallions and sweat stains on his shirt; a hyper guy who paced the room like he was on foot patrol (he must have believed the hype that all us inner-city kids were animals); one lady who did absolutely nothing with us while she opened her mail, sorted her bills, balanced her checkbook, and otherwise got her affairs in order (most students liked her); and another lady who taught nights at the community college, only her discipline was American history. Since Mr. Brook had gone, we hadn't learned anything. It was just like Flanders was back.

One day in homeroom I was given that familiar summons. I trekked to Bowman's office thinking I was about to be reamed for skipping school. Finally, he was going to do it—throw me in jail for truancy.

When I entered his robin's-egg blue office, I was surprised by his question. "How is he?"

How is he? I collapsed into his chair.

Concern? Sincerity?

No threats?

No bullying?

No ominous soothsaying about what a dead end my life will be if I flunk out of high school?

I caught my breath.

"They were able to stop the hemorrhaging," I said. "He's watching game shows."

That sluggish, cloudy afternoon, things were just as weird at home. There was no judge show blaring, it didn't smell like Funyuns, and I thought this must be what heaven was like.

Q was gone!

Oh, he left behind the clutter, but that I could tend to, and I did. I got out the happy broom and the happy dustpan and the happiest of all, my vacuum cleaner.

In the middle of my cleaning groove, the doorbell rang.

"Hi," Jeff said, dressed like he was auditioning for a boy band.

My bones froze. A cloud of fuzziness passed over my brain.

"How did you know where I live?" I asked.

"Steph'Annie told me. I hope you don't mind."

I would have brought him in, but the place was at that point only one-eighth clean.

"Let's go for a walk," I suggested.

I smelled not of lipstick and perfume but of Lysol and rug shampoo. Jeff had caught me in patched jeans and an old shirt. It was just as well that this, my first date ever, was impromptu. What was I planning to wear on that scheduled day? I didn't own anything yellow or pink. Everything I owned was brown or black, so what was the difference, right?

We walked farther into town and I talked about Mr. Brook.

"He must be a great teacher," Jeff said.

"He means everything to me," I confessed.

"Everything? I've never had a teacher that meant all that to me. I didn't even think that was possible. He's just your teacher, right?"

"Right," I said, which wasn't a lie, technically.

He touched the side of my face. "Here." He lifted a plant from a bag he'd been carrying. "I know it's awfully bare in those hospital rooms."

I pushed it back to him. "Jeff, I won't be going back."

"Why not?"

"He doesn't want me to visit him."

His eyebrows drew together, but then he said, "People get real batty in the hospital. A lot of guys of that generation—they don't like a lot of fanfare. He probably doesn't want students visiting him. He's got a family to come visit him."

"He doesn't have a family."

"Well, maybe he was just talking off the top of his head. Everybody wants visitors."

"Everybody?"

"You know the saying, no man is an island."

As we sat in the park, we couldn't help noticing the proliferation of canines. The dog-to-human ratio was nearly even. People walked precious little Fifi dogs, medium-sized Lassies, and great big Marmaduke dogs. Companionship abounded. I guess I could have taken solace in that, but unfortunately, from that park I had a direct view of Mr. Brook's building.

"Are you looking for something?" Jeff asked.

"No. I'm listening."

"No, you're not—" He turned so he could see what I was seeing, only to find an apartment building.

"That's his place."

"Must be nice." He nodded. "He must have a pretty good grip for a teacher."

"He's retired. He earned a lot in his old career."

Jeff shook his head. "You know way too much about this old dude. You better watch it before something happens."

Jeff's warning struck me as painfully funny. Suddenly, all I could think of was the last time I'd seen Mr. Brook. How weird and distant he was.

"Why don't we go somewhere else?" Jeff said. He said his apartment was not too far away and explained that it was a sublease and he had a roommate.

"What's your roommate like?" I asked, trying to get back to the present.

"Hardly there. He has a girl."

Jeff lived in a three-room apartment, in space not taken up by splayed CDs and Pringles cans. Not as meticulously tended as Mr. Brook's was, I'm sure, but dusted with some regularity.

Someone had left a clear bottle of orange juice on the table, with a bowl and a box of cornflakes.

I pointed. "This yours?"

"Yep."

"You're a cornflake eater?"

He squared off with me. "Yeah, you want to make something of it?"

"What I don't like about cornflakes is that they don't crackle. They just lie there."

"Exactly." He nodded, signifying that that was precisely what he liked about them.

He told me that he had moved here because it was close to New York City. But he was on cornflakes in Philly, and there was no cheaper cereal, so what would he be on in NYC?

He was originally from Kansas City, which he assured me was not in Kansas.

"Mo," he stated.

I didn't know what he was talking about.

He went on to say that he had actually been in community theater productions back in Missouri and presently he was a fill-in reenactment actor in the new Constitution Center on Fifth Street. Mostly, though, he went to auditions on a moment's notice.

"So you have to be ready to go the same day."

"Yep."

"Do you like that?" I asked.

He shrugged. "That's the game. A commercial can give you money that can float for a good couple of weeks."

"Weeks? Then what?"

"Then I audition again. The thing is to get momentum. Have them ask for you."

"That's always nice."

"Yeah. You know, I didn't even get that ape part."

"What ape part?"

"The children's play. The one I was up for when I met you. I was studying for it at the zoo."

"So that was for a play?"

"No, I always talk to orangutans." He grinned, then coaxed me, "Tell me more about yourself. I've done most of the talking."

"I don't have any hobbies."

"Sure you do. I saw you at the zoo."

"I was just visiting Dru."

"Dru?" he asked. "Is that her name?"

"His," I corrected him.

"Her," he insisted.

"His!"

Next thing I knew, he pulled a book from the shelf and paged through it to find a picture. He showed it to me.

"Male orangutans have these flaps on their face."

I studied the picture and its caption: sure enough, Jeff was right.

"I have to return all these to the library. I used them to study for my role."

"I guess Dru is a girl," I said, surprising myself with how disappointed I sounded. It wasn't like I'd ever seen a future between us.

"That could still work. Dru is one of those names that goes both ways, like Jessie."

"You don't understand," I mumbled. "I went to the primate center all the time to see him—"

"I don't understand? What's the big deal, so what? So he's a she? What are you, in love with an ape?" he asked, and laughed heartily.

Silently, I pleaded the Fifth. I went back to his books, which were mainly on acting.

"Who's Stanli—" I tried to sound the name out.

"Stanislavsky. He was this acting coach. He worked with all the greats. Marlon Brando. Marilyn Monroe."

"Marilyn Monroe was a great actress? I thought

she was just pretty." I flipped through the pages. "So what part are you up for next?"

"There's a dinner theater revival of *How to Succeed in Business Without Really Trying.*"

"A businessman? You?" I asked.

"And you can see me as an ape?" he asked me. "Hey, would you like to audition, too? There are a lot of girl parts."

"I would like to get a gig going, but something stable. No offense."

"No offense taken. Why do you think they usually put the word 'starving' before the word 'artist'?" He snapped his fingers. "I got it. I'll ask at the Rocket. Maybe there's an opening."

"You don't have to," I quickly said.

"I know I don't," he told me, and winked. "I want to. . . . Mind if I put on some music?"

"Music?" I asked, as if I'd never heard the word before.

He turned on the player, and I was surprised he listened to that fifties stuff at home, as well.

"Where would the world be without Leiber and Stoller?" he asked.

"Who are they?"

"Samara, they're playing now."

"They sing pretty good."

"This is the Drifters featuring Ben E. King. They're not singing."

"You just said—"

"Jerry Leiber and Mike Stoller were songwriters."

The song was called "Dance with Me."

Jeff spun me around and dipped me till my back ached. I felt his palm in the small of my back. It felt nice. I got to thinking that he could do anything.

And then he started to sing very flat, soullessly.

And then I thought, *Well, he can do almost everything.*

He spoke again about the songwriting duo and he reminded me of Mr. Brook in the way he lapsed into lecture. I learned that Leiber and Stoller wrote "Hound Dog" when they were only twenty years old, and later composed hits like "Jailhouse Rock," "Love Potion No. 9," and "On Broadway."

The song Jeff had put on was one of those shoop-shoop, doo-doo songs. I didn't mind the shoop-shoop, shoop-shoop-de-doop, but the doo-doos really got on my nerves. The actual lyrics were so simple they were practically transparent. "Dance with me, / Hold me tighter."

"I love this music," he told me. "You know, a hundred years from now at car shows, what will they have? Toyotas? Hyundais? Volvos? No, Cadillacs, Mustangs, Chevies. Rock and roll will never go out of style."

nineteen

The next day, Jeff set up an interview at the Rocket, and like magic I was a hostess. I was the most content minium-wage-earning American ever.

My uniform wasn't as corny as the poodle-skirted waitresses'. I got to wear my own jeans and a pink shirt with my name embroidered at the chest. Only they spelled it wrong, so for the first week I was Sahara.

Every tenth customer asked, "Were you named after the desert?"

Time galloped when I was at work. It seemed that no sooner did I punch in than I would look up and see that it was quitting time.

Every now and then someone would slip me a tip, like once these two Armani-suited guys came in with their briefcases and accordion folders and spreadsheets. When they were leaving, they asked me to hail them a cab, and I walked a few steps out the door and put up my hand.

The taller one placed a bill in my palm. I opened it and found a ten—not bad for two minutes of work. If only I could run into sixty guys like that. I could make three hundred dollars per hour.

I wouldn't mind being a hostess for the rest of my life. I would never want to be a waitress; that's too much of a long-term relationship. By being a hostess, I flitted in and out of the customers' lives. It never got deep. I never asked them searching questions like "Fries with that?" "Rare, medium, or well?" Just greet and seat, and I was done.

The few who came in testy I showed to the table with the wobbly leg.

On nights that both Jeff and I worked, he walked me home. Jeff always insisted we go the scenic route: what I knew as Broad Street, but postgentrification it was known as the Avenue of the Arts. One night he put his arms around me and drew me close.

He leaned over to kiss me, and I didn't lean back to avoid it. I leaned in a little, let his lips linger on mine. He was taller than me, but not by a whole lot.

We would always catch this percussionist on the street, a kid about Jeff's age. He didn't play a regular drum. Instead, he used pots and pans.

That night we stood and listened for a while.

Jeff gave him a dollar. "Got to support the arts."

That Friday, my favorite customers came in: Steph'Annie, Kath, and the text messager, Roxanne.

They took a booth, and when it was slow, Steph'Annie waved me over and patted the seat next to her.

"You look so cute!" Steph'Annie played with the flip in my hair as I sat down.

Chuck Berry's "Johnny B. Goode" was playing on the jukebox.

"This place is ridiculous!" Kath exclaimed.

"What's so ridiculous about it?" I asked.

"It's too nostalgic."

"What's so wrong about taking a stroll down memory lane?" Steph'Annie asked in her usual sunny voice.

"Like the fifties was such a great time? Memory lane? Segregation alone makes it worth the trip," Kath said sarcastically.

"If you feel that strongly about it, why do you come here?" Steph'Annie asked.

"I like the milk shakes," Kath told her.

Chuck's song ended and Jerry Lee Lewis played "Great Balls of Fire."

"I know you're going out with Jeff, but how's your other guy doing?" Steph asked me.

I played dumb. "Who?"

"You know who." She punched me on the arm. "The one with the je ne sais quoi. Old dude. Was he up, that last time you saw him?"

"I haven't seen him since he nearly cussed me out."

The text messager looked up from her phone and asked, "Really?"

"The nice old man didn't mean it, Samara."

"He told me to beat it, Steph'Annie."

Kath nodded. "That's the medication talking."

"Yeah, he probably didn't know what he was saying," Steph'Annie said.

"He was serious."

"You have to see him again," Steph'Annie insisted.

"No, she doesn't," Kath said flatly.

"You don't know the electricity," Steph'Annie said.

"You said he was seventy years old," Kath said.

"Age is just a number," Steph'Annie said.

Kath gestured to me. "She's freakin' fifteen—"

"He's her soul mate," Steph'Annie said.

"He's my what?" I asked.

"S-o-u-l m-a-t-e," Steph'Annie answered.

"Not if he's going to flip on her," Kath reasoned. "There's no need to get twisted over him."

"But the electricity—" Steph said.

"There's other fish in the sea, Samara." Kath turned to me.

"Samara, 'There's so many fish in the sea / That

only rise up in the sweat and smoke like mercury.' "
Steph'Annie let the words set in. "Elvis Costello."

"She means Presley," Kath corrected her.

They argued like cats over a ball of yarn. It was
Presley! Costello! Back and forth for the next few
moments. Steph'Annie had told me she had known
Kath all her life. They were cousins on her mother's
side. Blood relations work like that sometimes. I got
the feeling they could argue about anything but still
end up loving each other.

Luckily a customer came in, and I had an excuse
not to think of fish in the sea, primates in the zoo, or
buses passing by every twenty minutes.

"I got to get back to work," I told them.

Roxanne looked up from her phone for a split
second and smiled at me.

*A haze fills my bedroom from just one cigarette; it
curls in ribbons, and my mother bursts in. "When did
you start smoking?" she gasps.*

I play dumb. "What?"

She points. "In your hand."

"Oh, this . . . I don't really smoke. This is my first

time. Ever." As if on cue, I cough once. Then again and again. She rushes over, takes me in her arms, and pats me furiously on the back.

Weeping, she says, "We've grown so far apart. When did you get a job, Samara?"

"Two weeks ago."

"And who's this Jeff who keeps calling?"

"A boy I'm seeing."

Tears are thick in her eyes. "You have a job, you're seeing a boy, and you smoke."

She sounds so warm. So loving. I have to bring her up to speed. I hold her and confess, "I have a crush on a seventy-two-year-old man and I visit the primate center!"

The preceding sequence was a fantasy. It never happened. In those Q-less days, Mom wasn't drawn closer to me. In her hours off, she took to television. She especially liked to watch infomercials. One night, there was one about speed-reading techniques. It promised you could get through books in a flash, and thus you could watch more TV, preferably more infomercials.

Mom barely acknowledged my presence as I walked past her to the kitchen to reheat some Rocket food (a burger and onion rings—it beat microwaving popcorn).

Still, this Q-free zone was pure. If I wasn't where I wanted to be, at least I wasn't back where I had been.

twenty

Some say love is like a light switch: it goes on and off. However, I believe that love is much more nuanced. Love is a clock. When you are in half love, it's six straight up. If you are not in love, it's quarter to three. When he starts to grow on you, it's a little past nine.

Jeff called at 9:15 p.m. with word that he had landed a role. He would have two whole lines in a chain restaurant commercial.

"That's great news!" I exclaimed.

Jeff went through more details of how he nailed the competition to the wall with his delivery of:

"There's nothing in the world like a toasted submarine sandwich" and "Mmm—that's good."

I laughed.

"We'll have to go out and celebrate this weekend."

"They paid you already?"

"No, but what the hell, let's just celebrate."

"Okay."

We decided on Saturday, since we were both off that night. Then he told me he had to go. He wanted to call his mother.

After I hung up, he danced in my heart till ten-thirty, when I went to bed.

That night I stared out my window and looked at my old friend, the moon. Though alone, she was surrounded by stars. They kept her company all night long.

The next morning in first period, Flanders was back, sporting long, wide black blotches on her arm. She had contracted this sort of flesh-eating staph infection from a cut-rate manicure salon.

It was the oddest sensation. She was one of

those people who disappeared, like oar ripples through water.

It had been a good five weeks since I'd last seen her. Had I missed her? Had anyone missed her?

Flanders who?

She picked up right where she'd left off. In fact, she began diagramming the same sentence she had left with: "The writer uses a comma to set off a definition, a restatement, or extra information."

"Bring back the old dude," Steph'Annie said loudly enough for Flanders to hear.

Flanders's eyebrows knitted together. "What are you talking about?"

Steph'Annie didn't follow up.

The AP wannabe pulled out his notebook.

A girl up front began painting her fingernails. The smell of the acetone filled the room immediately.

Next period, Rosetti's "hot Italian temper" was acting up at Larry Carlson. Rosetti got red in the face, and even from my third-row post I could see his pupils dilating.

Larry Carlson didn't have a book.

"Why didn't you bring your book?

"Where is your book?

"You call yourself a student and you don't have your book!"

Larry had his head low, trying to look inconspicuous. One thing was for sure: with his lax attitude, Larry wouldn't have a heart attack anytime soon. Rosetti might. He had a wedding ring, so I was sure he had a wife and kids—I couldn't imagine breaking the news to his family if he did up and go into cardiac arrest over a student not having a book.

"Why is it so difficult for you to do something so simple?"

I had to turn away. Through the barred windows, I eyed the tops of trees and their quivering leaves. Birds twittered.

I raised my hand and asked if I could use the bathroom.

Mr. Rosetti barked, "Go!"

When I got to the hall, I embarked on my Houdini maneuver.

* * *

I was back to my old ways, heading straight for the zoo. Dru's soulful eyes lit up when I marched up to her cage. But before I buddied up to her, I wanted to get this one thing off my chest.

"You could have told me you were a chick," I said nonverbally.

Dru's eyes widened. *"I tried."*

My eyes narrowed. *"You led me on for weeks!"*

Dru made a sad face, and I realized that I had scolded her enough. I changed the subject. *"I want to tell you that I met someone. You know him! He was here. Talk about coincidences. Remember the guy with the midlength dreads flailing like he was having a fit? Well, turns out he's a Method actor."*

Dru looked at me with disappointment. *"So that's why you haven't been by to see me!"*

"That's not why." My eyes also told her about my part-time job at Rocket and the blessed departure of Q. I asked her what was new with her.

She told me that she'd just turned four years old. *"Happy birthday, Dru."*

After she was all caught up, I turned to leave.

"Wait," I sensed her cry out to me.

I faced her.

Her eyes asked, *"Can't we be friends?"*

"Of course," my eyes answered. For old times' sake, I placed my lips to the glass, and Dru followed suit and pressed. I felt a warmth from my chin to my nose.

It was still early, and I knew if I hustled I could get to the hospital before afternoon visiting hours were done.

I was going to see Mr. Brook whether he liked it or not.

There was a cluster of people waiting for the elevator, which was on the twelfth floor. I couldn't wait. I turned to where there was a shorter line and snuck into the service elevator to the fourteenth floor with a moaning man on a gurney. He was sandwiched between two interns, who both spoke about last night's basketball game.

"The Pistons really cleaned the floor with the Sixers, didn't they?" the shorter one asked.

The supine man groaned again.

They wheeled him out at the tenth floor. For the

rest of the ride, I was alone with my pounding heart and my galloping thoughts.

At floor fourteen, the door opened, and I leaped out. I ran like an impulsive heroine from a romance novel toward her forbidden love. I didn't have the kind of hair that flowed behind me, nor did I wear that kind of long billowing dress, but the intent was there.

I ran right into his room, only to find an empty bed.

I rushed into the hall and waved down an orderly. He had round shoulders and a droopy uniform.

"What happened to the man who was in this room?" I asked.

"He's been gone a week," he said.

My heart gave a lurch; I took a step back.

My body went so cold, I was surprised my heart didn't stop beating. After a long silence, I asked, "Gone where?"

My question went to no one in particular because the orderly had already gone off down the hall, busy with his duties.

I ran to the nurses' station and found a woman

in her forties with caked-on makeup. She looked a lot like the intake attendant from ICU.

"I have to know what happened to Mr. Jerome Halbrook," I said.

The nurse made no motion toward her notes or the computer. "Have to?" she asked. "Why is that? Who are you?"

"I'm—I'm—" I stumbled, unable to get the daughter or granddaughter or niece lie going.

"Don't you know who you are?" she asked me.

"Look, can you help me?" I pleaded.

"Not until you can tell me what relation you are to that patient. HIPAA laws prohibit—"

She was still rattling on about HIPAA, whatever that is, as I walked away, suddenly exhausted. Suddenly empty. I didn't know how I found the strength to walk, to put one foot in front of the other.

Where was Mr. Brook? Was he alive? Was he dead? What was I supposed to assume with no one giving me a straight answer?

I ran back down the hall, where the orderly was now sweeping, and asked again. "What happened to Mr. Jerome Halbrook?"

"I told you, miss, he's gone from here," he said, and he went right back to his sweeping. Sweeping at a time like this. All around me, people were chatting on the phone, scribbling notations.

Before I knew it I was on ground level, then outside waiting at the bus stop. There was one way to know.

I got on the bus. The driver drove, and the world just spun on its axis like nothing substantial had changed.

People scrambled for a place. I stood. What difference did sitting in a red seat with blue trim make? The bus pitched its way down Walnut Street. There was no comfort to be found with all the honking and screeching.

The bus jerked its way deeper into the city. I was heading for Rittenhouse Square. His spot. I thought of the vigil Steph'Annie and I'd held there.

I stood and weaved my way from the middle of the bus to the front. I was close when I got off: his apartment was a mere two blocks away.

He had to be there.

Walking in the opposite direction, I encountered

cell phones ringing, leashed dogs barking, and traffic cops whistling.

I just had to see something of his one more time. I spun on my heels and began sprinting toward his building. As I approached, I searched the fifth-floor windows. I saw a figure moving. The light was on.

A man in a gray warm-up suit was checking his mailbox. He held the door open for me. I slid in, bypassing the elevator. I took the stairs.

Panting, I crept toward his door. I heard movement inside. I smelled flavored coffee. Vanilla almond? No. Amaretto? No. I felt the door before knocking.

All at once, it opened.

I saw him.

twenty-one

"You're alive!" I exclaimed.

His eyes rested full on my face. "Sharp as ever."

Calm and steady, he returned to folding a white shirt and placing it in a steel trunk.

"What are you doing?" I asked.

"Packing."

"I thought you were dead."

He stopped folding for a moment and said, "I'm not."

I stepped inside, caught my breath. My eyes took in his apartment and boxes stacked by the window. "The people at the hospital almost had me believing you were dead."

"They're overworked and underpaid. They can't be expected to get everything right," he said.

I got the joke, but how could I laugh?

"I hope they gave you the letter," Mr. Brook said.

A letter? I couldn't even get my mind to process that. I looked around with my head still swimming from the run and lamented that I would never know how he had laid out his apartment. The walls were bare and beige. I had missed it.

"Samara, did you get the letter I left for you?"

"No, I didn't," I said plaintively.

He sighed. "Well, would you like something? I have coffee on."

"No thank you."

"You don't like coffee?"

"I don't want any. What did the letter say?"

"I can't believe they didn't give you the letter. I wrote you an apology for being so rude the last time we saw each other. It said everything. It explained that I've been in remission for the last five years, and I thought I was home free. So when they said it has come back, I felt so defeated. I didn't want you to see me like that."

"So it was better that you push me away."

"I'm sorry that it seemed like that. Well, that was what the letter said, more or less, but in better words. . . . No one wants to be seen at their weakest."

"I could never see you as weak."

"Samara, everyone has weakness and doubt. It's easy to put up a brave front when you know there'll be a happy ending, but I didn't know how things would turn out. And all that talk about hope seemed as far away as the moon."

"I could never see you as weak, Mr. Brook," I repeated, spilling my pet name for him.

He nodded and smiled a little. "Are you sure I can't offer you something to drink? Do you want to sit down?"

I shook my head and looked at his luggage. "Where are you going?"

"I'm going home."

"Home?"

"Columbia, South Carolina. Maybe I'll even get my accent back. Then I'm off."

"Off?"

"To the islands."

"Which ones?" I asked.

"Greece. You know, they have over a thousand there."

"That does sound like something. But are these Greek islands known for great medical care?"

"That doesn't matter. I want to see them, Samara. I've always wanted to. So many years ago, I had them circled on a map. Funny, how sixty years goes by like a long weekend."

"I hope you're exaggerating."

"The older you get, the faster it moves. You mark my words. . . . Well, they ought to be around here any minute now."

"They?"

"The Goodwill people. They're about the only ones who'd want an old man's bed."

"Don't you plan to sleep when you get down there?" I asked him.

"I hate shipping. Nothing's ever in the right condition when it arrives. Some things are always altered. It's better to start—"

"Clean?" I interrupted.

He nodded. "Yes, clean."

I looked out the window to where an office building stretched, punching into the sky. Dusk was falling.

He was taking only a moderate-sized steel trunk, one bag, and a cup.

He puttered about the room with the energy of a toddler. Him just out of the hospital. Shouldn't he be sitting? Resting? Conserving his energy for all those days on the beaches? That long, languid eternity staring at the neon blue skies with the same radiant eyes with which he'd looked at me that first day. That day when I'd had nothing and he'd given me everything.

"You have the right idea. I'm sure Southern life will agree with you," I muttered. "I hope you have a safe trip. I hope no weirdos sit next to you. You know what I mean. The people who just want to talk and talk and talk." I could have gone on forever like a weirdo myself but my mouth went dry.

I'd gone for the door in the hopes of saving both him and me more embarrassment when I remembered. "I still have your book. *Immortal Poetry*."

"Good."

"I want to read it again. And again. And then again and again."

"Take your time, Samara."

"Right," I said, whirling again to leave.

"Samara," he called.

I looked back, my eyes moist, my body having quakes, miniquakes, little emotional tremors in my limbs.

"I'm going to miss you," he said.

My eyes welled up. Tears tumbled down my cheeks.

He reached out his hand. Of course, I took it and held it.

His hand felt so warm, it was like being kissed.

I stepped away first and turned, feeling his eyes on my back.

I clutched the knob and opened the door smoothly. I continued to walk, placing one foot in front of the other, as I'd been doing since I was ten months old. But it was harder now. I went down the steps. Head down.

I dried my eyes on the heel of my hand. Taking

the stairs one heavy, lonely step at a time, I came to the front entrance and stepped outside.

I patted my jacket for my cigarettes. I took one out and put it in my mouth, then spun around.

He had come to the window. His blue eyes sent invisible sparks to me even from this distance. He was holding a cigarette. This cancer patient was about to light up. Defiantly. Earnestly.

He smoked as I watched from five stories below. I closed my eyes and smelled the world. Strangely, it now smelled of possibilities.

I shook my head and put the cigarette away. My dry eyes were open now. I turned back around and began walking.

The rest of my life eased before me like ice cream in July.

poems mr. brook read

TO HIS COY MISTRESS
by Andrew Marvell

Had we but world enough, and time,
This coyness, lady, were no crime.
We would sit down and think which way
To walk, and pass our long love's day;
Thou by the Indian Ganges' side
Shouldst rubies find; I by the tide
Of Humber would complain. I would
Love you ten years before the Flood;
And you should, if you please, refuse
Till the conversion of the Jews.
My vegetable love should grow
Vaster than empires, and more slow.
An hundred years should go to praise
Thine eyes, and on thy forehead gaze;
Two hundred to adore each breast,
But thirty thousand to the rest;
An age at least to every part,
And the last age should show your heart.
For, lady, you deserve this state,
Nor would I love at lower rate.

But at my back I always hear
Time's winged chariot hurrying near;
And yonder all before us lie
Deserts of vast eternity.
Thy beauty shall no more be found,
Nor, in thy marble vault, shall sound
My echoing song; then worms shall try
That long preserv'd virginity,
And your quaint honour turn to dust,
And into ashes all my lust.
The grave's a fine and private place,
But none I think do there embrace.

Now therefore, while the youthful hue
Sits on thy skin like morning dew,
And while thy willing soul transpires
At every pore with instant fires,
Now let us sport us while we may;
And now, like am'rous birds of prey,
Rather at once our time devour,
Than languish in his slow-chapp'd power.
Let us roll all our strength, and all
Our sweetness, up into one ball;
And tear our pleasures with rough strife
Thorough the iron gates of life.
Thus, though we cannot make our sun
Stand still, yet we will make him run.

AFTER GREAT PAIN, A FORMAL FEELING COMES
by Emily Dickinson

After great pain, a formal feeling comes—
The Nerves sit ceremonious, like Tombs—
The stiff Heart questions was it He,
that bore,
And Yesterday, or Centuries before?

The Feet, mechanical, go round—
Of Ground, or Air, or Ought—
A Wooden way
Regardless grown,
A Quartz contentment, like a stone—

This is the Hour of Lead—
Remembered, if outlived,
As Freezing persons, recollect the Snow—
First—Chill—then Stupor—then the
letting go—

LIFE IS FINE
by Langston Hughes

I went down to the river,
I set down on the bank.
I tried to think but couldn't,
So I jumped in and sank.

I came up once and hollered!
I came up twice and cried!
If that water hadn't a been so cold
I might've sunk and died.

But it was Cold in that water! It was cold!

I took the elevator
Sixteen floors above the ground.
I thought about my baby
And thought I would jump down.

I stood there and I hollered!
I stood there and I cried!
If it hadn't a-been so high
I might've jumped and died.

But it was High up there! It was high!

So since I'm still here livin',
I guess I will live on.
I could've died for love—
But for livin' I was born

Though you may hear me holler,
And you may see me cry—
I'll be dogged, sweet baby,
If you gonna see me die.

Life is fine! Fine as wine! Life is fine!

About the Author

A Philadelphia native and a Virgo,
Allison Whittenberg studied dance for years
before switching her focus to writing. She has
an MA in English from the University of
Wisconsin and enjoys traveling to places like
the Caribbean and Russia. Her first novel,
Sweet Thang, is available from Yearling Books.